The Dogs of War Series
Volume 4

Claws of Steel

Also by Leo Kessler and available from
Spellmount Publishers in
The Dogs of War Series

THE
DOGS OF WAR SERIES
VOLUME 4

CLAWS OF STEEL

by

Leo Kessler

SPELLMOUNT
Staplehurst

British Library Cataloguing in Publication Data:
A catalogue record for this book is available
from the British Library

Copyright © Charles Whiting 1974, 1986, 2004

ISBN 1-86227-267-0

First published in the UK in 1974

This edition first published in the UK in 2004 by
Spellmount Limited
The Village Centre
Staplehurst
Kent TN12 0BJ

Tel: 01580 893730
Fax: 01580 893731
E-mail: enquiries@spellmount.com
Website: www.spellmount.com

1 3 5 7 9 8 6 4 2

Printed in Great Britain by
Bookmarque Ltd, Croydon, Surrey

'When the order is given, you will drive forward with the greatest tank armies ever assembled in the history of warfare . . . crushing the life out of the Soviet serpent with two huge claws of steel.' *Adolf Hitler to his generals, May 1943*.

A SHORT GLOSSARY OF WOTAN TERMS

Asparagus Tarzan	Weakling
Golden Pheasant	Nazi Party official
Popov, Ivan	Russian soldier
Spaghetti-eater, Macaroni	Italian
Greenbeak, wet-tail	Raw Recruit
Ami	American
Base Stallion	Rear-area soldier, 'base-wallah'
Bone-mender	Doctor
Warm brother	Homosexual
Kitchen-bull	Army cook
Field-Mattress	German Army female auxiliary
Tin	Decorations
Throatache	Knight's Cross of the Iron Cross
Cancer stick	Cigarette
Dice-beakers	Jackboots
Marie, green-leaves	Money, banknotes
Wood in front of the door	Big bosom
Old Man	Tinned meat
Giddi-up soup	Horsemeat soup
Reeperbahn-equalizer	Brass knuckles
Stubble-hopper	Infantryman

ONE: THE GREAT PLAN

'The whole of Germany's tired. Heaven, arse and twine, we're fighting half the world after all! And that's exactly why we must be hard. The German soldier has to be so hard that he is the match for any two Tommies, Amis or Ivans – and the SS man has to be twice as hard as the ordinary Wehrmacht stubble-hopper!' *Major Geier, CO SS Assault Battalion WOTAN to Capt. v. Dodenburg, June 1943.*

ONE

The Mercedes swung out of the Mauer Forest on to the road to Rastenburg. Immediately it picked up speed. On either side the spring gale was ripping at the branches of the ancient beeches and whipping up the surface of Lake Mauer into white caps.

But the high ranking officers in the Mercedes, the sombre field-grey of their uniforms relieved only by the crimson stripe of the staff down the sides of their trousers, had no eyes for the East Prussian scenery this spring day. The situation at the Russian Front was too serious. Stalingrad had fallen and a quarter of a million German soldiers had shambled off into the Russian cages. Now they knew the Führer must make the right decision, because if he didn't soon, the whole Eastern Front could well break under the tremendous weight the Red Army was bringing to bear on it.

Colonel-General Model's car stopped at Gate 1 to Special Area 1 of the 'Wolf's Lair'. The SS guards saluted rigidly. But even though the red-faced General with the monocle squeezed into his right eye was well known at the HQ, they insisted on seeing his identity card. With a muffled curse he passed it over to the massive Lieutenant in charge of the guard and stared straight ahead at the sombre headquarters hidden in the East Prussian Forest. What had General Jodl once called the place? Half monastery and half concentration camp? It damned well looked like it.

Satisfied with his ID card, the massive SS officer clicked to attention once again and ordered the guard to lift the red-and-white striped pole. Colonel-General Model could pass through. One by one the grey camouflaged Mercedes followed. Drop a bomb on this road now, Model thought sourly as the convoy formed up again, and that would be end of German Army. For all its key leaders were present in the convoy – Manstein, Guderian, Hoth – summoned from all over the vast Eastern Front to hear what the former Corporal in the Bavarian Infantry had planned for them.

But there was little chance of an enemy bomb hitting Adolf Hitler's HQ, Model told himself, even if the Tommies had possessed a bomber capable of flying so far. The low concrete huts, their flat roofs turned into gardens, were perfectly hidden in the tall beeches. They'd be impossible to see from the air. And as for a land-based attack, the Wolf's Lair was hermetically sealed off from the outer world by layer after layer of minefields and roadblocks, defended by the elite of the 'Bodyguard Division'. Whatever else they said about the Führer, Model concluded, he was no fool when it came to looking after his own safety. The Ivans or the Tommies would need an army to break into this place.

A few moments later the convoy of high-ranking officers swung by the last barrier, inside which the Führer's own Alsatian bitch Blondi ran around freely, ready to go for the genitals of any unauthorised person, and halted outside the Leader's own hut in which today's vital conference was to be held.

Jodl, Hitler's pale-faced clever Chief-of-Staff, received them at the door and ushered into the map room, where the top secret maps were already laid out on the big oak table.

'You may be seated gentlemen,' he said and indicated the high-legged wooden stools around the table. 'Of course no smoking in the Führer's presence. Remember that Guderian.'

He looked at Colonel-General Guderian, the father of the 'Blitzkrieg', and the others laughed politely, for they knew

12

the hot-tempered panzer leader liked his cheap ten pfennig cigars.

'You may help yourself to soft drinks.' He indicated the bottles on the table. 'For those of you who are so inclined, the Führer's barley water is over there. But there'll be nothing strong, I'm afraid, until after the conference. However you can—'

'Jodl,' Model interrupted him in irritation, 'we've heard all this before. Before the Führer comes, brief us quickly. Heaven, arse and twine, Jodl, you know we don't want to be caught with our breeches down when he starts asking those awkward damned questions of his!'

Jodl's pale cunning eyes gleamed with unusual animation for him.

'I can tell you this, Model. You and Hoth, and naturally you too, Field Marshall,' he bowed his head politely in Manstein's direction, 'will be getting the biggest job of your whole careers. What the Führer is going to propose to you will be the most tremendous—'

'Gentlemen,' Field Marshall Keitel's harsh Prussian voice broke in to the discussion, 'the Führer!'

They stiffened to attention immediately like a bunch of young recruits meeting their drill sergeant for the first time. Keitel, as wooden-faced and impassively stupid as ever, had flung open the door to admit Adolf Hitler. He flashed a quick look at them and then barked, 'Heil Hitler!'

'Heil Hitler!' The handful of men, who had commanded Germany's military destiny for the last three years, flung up their right arms in the Roman salute.

Dramatically Adolf Hitler stood there and gave each one of them a long searching look with those hypnotic eyes of his, peering into their hard soldiers' faces, as if he hoped to see something there, known only to himself. Manstein, clever

13

and cynical, and probably half-Jewish[1] for all he knew; Guderian, awkward but brilliant, a general he'd already sacked once, whom he could not do without; Model, gross, a heavy drinker, but a lion in defence; and Hoth, grey-haired and quiet, but so good that he was going to entrust him with the greatest tank army ever assembled in the history of battle. Finally he broke off his scrutiny of their faces.

'Gentlemen,' he said quietly, 'you may be seated.'

He gave them a few moments to settle themselves on the hard wooden stools, then got down to business at once.

'Gentlemen, I know what some of you are thinking. We have suffered a severe setback at Stalingrad, I must admit that. Some of you think therefore, that we should go over to the defensive.'

He looked at them challengingly, as if he expected them to agree, but even Guderian managed to keep his mouth shut and fix his angry eyes on the maps in front of him.

'But we will not go over to the defensive. That would be playing into the Bolsheviks' hands, and I am not going to play any game prescribed for me by that Yiddish clique which rules Soviet Russia. No.' He paused and thrust out his jaw aggressively, as if he were giving one of his great dramatic speeches at the annual Nuremburg Party Rally. 'Gentlemen, I am proud to announce to you that National Socialist Germany will not just be content to hold what it has conquered in these last eighteen months in Russia. National Socialist Germany will go over to the attack.' He brought his clenched fist down on the table hard. 'In three months' time, gentlemen, by the first of July 1943 at the latest, your armies will march east once again – and they will march to victory, final victory!'

Even their rigid military training could not prevent them

1. Manstein's real name was von Lewinski, supposedly a Jewish name (transl.)

14

gasping with surprise. Manstein's habitual slightly bored look vanished from his long face, as if it had been wiped off by an invisible hand.

Hitler smiled slightly, pleased with the effect his words had had. Then his face grew hard again.

'Gentlemen, this summer two great German armies will go over to the offensive – an offensive of decisive importance. One which must end in swift and final success. Those armies will be given the best formations, the best weapons, the best ammunition National Socialist Germany can provide – and that means the best in the world.' His dark eyes blazed with some inner fire. 'Victory at Kursk will be a beacon for the whole world!'

'*Kursk*,' Model breathed to himself. So that was it!

Hitler paused for breath before indicating they should come and look at the centre map. There was a hasty scraping of stools as they followed his command.

'You can see, gentlemen, that the Bolsheviks had cut a huge bulge into our front here around Kursk. That bulge presents a tremendous danger to our whole Eastern Front. It is from there that they will undoubtedly launch their own summer offensive which could well split our forces.'

The generals, bent over the big map, nodded their heads in agreement. Although they'd disagreed with the former corporal about strategy often enough in the past, they knew he was completetly right about the overwhelming danger presented by the Kursk salient.

'If we can attack first, gentlemen,' Hitler continued, 'not only will we be able to cripple the Bolsheviks' offensive power and protect our own front, but we shall be able to crash right into their rear. After Stalingrad they will not be expecting us to take the offensive, believe you me, I feel it in my bones. We shall take them off their guard.'

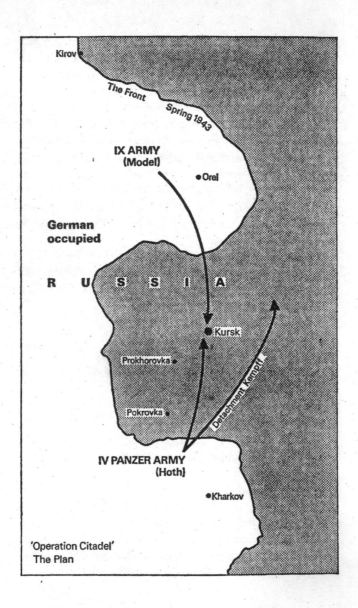

Kirov

The Front

Spring 1943

IX ARMY
(Model)

● Orel

German
occupied

R   U   S   S   I   A

● Kursk

Prokhorovka ●

Pokrovka ●

Detachment Kempff

IV PANZER ARMY
(Hoth)

● Kharkov

'Operation Citadel'
The Plan

'But my Führer,' Model said, before anyone else could protest, 'where are we to get the men?'

Hitler looked at the bemonocled general triumphantly. 'I expected you to ask that question, Model.' He turned to Jodl, his chief-of-staff. 'Jodl perhaps you would be good enough to detail our resources in case there are others present who doubt our ability to carry out the new offensive.'

Model flushed a deep red but did not say anything as all attention turned to Jodl.

Jodl was in his element. He had never been happy at the front; his greatest love was the staff, where the human element was reduced to a series of numbers or a red line on a graph.

'Gentlemen, since Stalingrad we have built up the greatest force assembled ever by the Wehrmacht. In the first line of attack we will have fifty divisions, sixteen of them panzer or motorised. Those divisions will contain nine hundred thousand men with ten thousand guns and three thousand tanks. They will be suported by 2,000 aircraft and a further twenty divisions in reserve, composed of—' Without a single glance at the notes held in his slim, well-manicured fingers, he rattled off statistic after statistic, while his fellow general officers listened to his exposé with ever-increasing awe. 'In short, gentlemen,' he concluded his brilliant summary of the forces available for the attack, 'the workers and civilian authorities of National Socialist Germany are putting the most powerful weapon known to the world in your hands, knowing that the Greater General Staff of the German Reich will not fail them in its use.'

He stopped and let the veiled threat sink in, but they overheard the threat; they were too bemused by the tremendous number of men and weapons that Hitler seemed to have conjured up from nowhere for this great new surprise summer offensive.

'My God, Jodl,' Model breathed, the monocle popping out of his right eye, the Führer's presence completely forgotten with the shock of it all, 'where in the devil's name did you get such numbers from?'

'I can tell you, Colonel-General!' Hitler said, exuberantly. 'From the sacrifice and will to victory of our German folk-comrades.[2] They are prepared to toil for eighteen hours a day on pitiful rations, subjected as they are to the terror raids of those Anglo-American air gangsters – and send their seventeen-year-old sons to war too – so that the Greater German Reich may achieve its great victory. 'Hitler's voice rose, the lock of unruly black hair fell over his forehead and little flecks of foam had collected at the sides of his mouth. 'For you, the Battle of Stalingrad was a defeat. But for me it was a kind of victory. Yes, a victory!'

He looked at them challengingly. 'For Stalingrad rallied this nation. Just as Dunkirk put the decadent English behind that drunken Jewish sot Churchill, Stalingrad has placed Germany behind me. Now the German Folk know it is march or croak as we used to say in the infantry in the old war. Now it is prepared to devote its very last bit of energy – its very life blood – into this fight for survival. My folk comrades know what victory at Kursk must mean for National Socialist Germany.'

He struck his padded chest almost angrily, his guttural Austrian voice rising even more hysterically, as he cried to his awed generals:

'Our armour will be concentrated in two great armies on either side of the salient. You, Model, will get the Ninth Army in the north. You, Hoth, the Fourth Panzer Army in the south. And know this, Hoth, I'm entrusting you with my elite, my SS panzer divisions.' His eyes bored into those of the white-haired tank commander.

2. National Socialist term for the ordinary citizens of the Third Reich (transl.)

18

'I'm very appreciative of the honour, my Führer,' Hoth stammered hastily. 'I am sure that I shall—'

His words faltered into nothing. Hitler was not listening. His hands held wide apart, he roared at them.

'When the order is given, you, Model, and you, Hoth, will drive forward with the greatest tank armies ever assembled in the history of warfare. You will take the Bolsheviks by complete surprise, smashing into them with your armour,' he brought his hands together abruptly, 'crushing the life out of the Soviet serpent with . . . with,' almost desperately he sought for the right words, *'with two huge claws of steel . . .'*

TWO

Sergeant Schulze of the SS Battalion Wotan[1] gave one of his celebrated farts. It was long-drawn out, and not unmusical. But the other NCOs of the First Company, stretched out in the long grass around him listening to Captain von Dodenburgh's lecture on the new Tiger tank, were obviously feeling as lazy as he was. They contented themselves with a polite titter at the burly Hamburger's attemps to amuse them on this hot June day.

The First Company's comedian was not offended. As he sat there with the flies buzzing around lazily in the heat, he felt happy with the world. The Battalion had not been in action for three months now; County Leader Schmeer's wife Waltraut cooked the best Schnitzel in the whole of Westphalia – though unfortunately she demanded a bit of meat from him in return; and her maid Heidi had the biggest pair

1. SS Assault Battalion Wotan, commanded by Major Geier, commonly known as the 'Vulture', formed in 1938, with active service in Poland, Belgium, the Channel and Russia. See Leo Kessler *SS Panzer Battalion* and *Death's Head* for further details.

19

of lungs it had ever been his good fortune to fondle – and he'd fondled plenty of big knockers in his twenty-seven years. He yawned mightily and tried to concentrate on the Company Commander's lecture about the Tiger.

'Those of you who were fortunate to serve with the Battalion in Russia,' he nodded to Sergeant Metzger, the Battalion's senior NCO, seated next to him, 'will remember that our Mark IVs armed with the short 75mm was not much of a match for the Popov's T-34.[2] The shells bounced off the damned thing's glacis plate like golf balls.' Von Dodenburg wiped the sweat off his bronzed face and frowned at the memory. 'But it's going to be different with this baby.' He tapped the sectional drawing of the Tiger pinned on the blackboard behind him. 'The Mark VI's 88 is the best gun in the world and the Tiger will carry enough ammo to see off a whole Popov tank brigade – 92 rounds of 88 and 5,700 for the two m.g.s. Here in the turret-co-axial of course – and down here next to the driver.'

He paused and pushing back his cap with its death's head insignia to reveal hair bleached to tow by the sun. 'In due course, you'll all be able to see for yourselves when the factories start delivery. For the time being, however, do you know what—'

'I do, sir,' Schulze interrupted him, knowing that his special position in the Battalion as its comedian and only non-commissioned holder of the Knight's Cross enabled him to take liberties. He grinned.

'I know what I'd like to do, sir – sink a nice foaming litre of beer! My mouth feels like the third-class waiting room at Hamburg Main Station!' He licked his dry lips mightily to emphasise his thirst and looked cheekily at von Dodenburg.

The handsome young company commander laughed.

2. The most common Soviet tank used on on the Eastern Front between 1941–1945 (transl.)

'Typical Schulze,' he said without rancour. 'Always thinking of his creature comforts. You're getting soft up here in Westphalia. Too much beer and too much Schnitzel. God knows what'll happen when we have to fight the Ivans again.'

'The way I feel now, sir,' Schulze replied, 'I'll just open my trap and breathe on 'em. I'm so dry and my breath's so hot, that it'll shrivel the Popovs up like a flame-thrower!'

Sergeant Metzger looked at the other NCO angrily. 'Just because he's got the crappy throatache, he thinks he can get away with murder,' he mumbled.

Von Dodenburg ignored him. He looked around the sweating red-faced NCOs sitting in the parched grass and then said: 'All right, you heroes. That'll be enough for today.'

Hastily Metzger sprang to his feet. Despite the June heat, he was dressed as if he were about to go on the Führer's Birthday Parade, his burly chest covered in decorations. He even had his 'monkey's swing' [3] dangling from his shoulder.

'Group – group attention!' he bellowed, as if they were a thousand metres away and not ten. He swung the officer a tremendous salute. 'Permission to dismiss, sir?' he barked.

Casually Captain von Dodenburg touched his hand to his cap. 'Granted, Metzger. Dismiss the men.'

Slowly von Dodenburg and Schulze walked back towards their billets, situated in the shadow of Paderborn's ancient Gothic cathedral, while the younger NCOs followed them at a respectful distance, not wishing to infringe on the conversation of these two men who had been fighting together since 1939.

'What do you make of it, sir, then?' Schulze asked, when he was sure that none of the others were listening.

'Make of what, you rogue?'

3. SS slang for the sharpshooter's lanyard, awarded to first-class shots (transl.)

21

'The new tank and everything?'

Captain von Dodenburg shrugged. 'We're getting a new tank, that's all Schulze.'

'Come on, sir,' Schulze persisted. 'Anybody with all his cups in his cupboard knows we're the Führer's fire-brigade. Wherever there's a blaze, off we go to put it out.'

'You're right – as always, Schulze.'

Schulze ignored the irony and waited.

'But if you took time to read the papers instead of feeding your face at County Leader Schmeer's – and undoubtedly doing other disreputable things which I don't want to know about – you would know that there is no blaze at the moment, especially on the Eastern Front. Marshal Mud's taken over from Marshal Winter. Not a damned thing is moving at the front at the moment.'

'Then when are we going to start the blaze?' Schulze persisted.

'Why the urgency, Schulze? I am surprised at you. I didn't realise you'd become a glory-hunter,' von Dodenburg joked.

'Me a glory-hunter,' the Hamburger said dourly. 'I've had a noseful – right up to here.' He drew a line under his big nose with his forefinger. 'But you take it from me, sir. Time is running out. I spent my last leave in Hamburg and there wasn't much of Barmbek where my old man lives left. The Tommies are knocking the shit out of the place and they're keeping it up in spite of what those glamour boys of the Luftwaffe can—'

'The Führer knows all about that. He'll fix the shitty Tommies, believe you me.' It was Metzger, who had caught up with them, the secret sectional plan of the new tank clasped importantly under his arm.

Captain von Dodenburg, his face suddenly serious at Schulze's mention of the hammering his hometown was tak-

22

ing, nodded. 'Yes, Metzger, you're right,' he said slowly. 'We can always rely on the Führer.'

Schulze said nothing as they began to march across the cobbled Cathedral square, he caught the look of uncertainty on the Captain's face. 'Yeah mate,' he told himself grimly, 'yer growing up at last, aren't yer. Yer learning that those crappy Tommies and Amis have got us by the short, black and curlies, Captain von Dodenburg . . .'

Captain von Dodenburg walked slowly and thoughtfully towards the evacuated school which had been turned into the Officers' Casino [4] when they had moved into the provincial Catholic town three months before. It was pleasant now in the shade of the twin towers and the bells were ringing melodiously, but he could not quite shake off the mood engendered by Schulze's remark just before they had parted.

He was right, of course. The Homeland was hard pressed by the enemy air gangsters. His own Berlin had suffered badly over these last months and his aged father, the General, had been forced to retire, much against his will, to his country estate in East Prussia, where he had set about raising a local defence immediately 'in case the Popovs come'. Though there was very little possibility of that. But it wasn't the bombing that worried von Dodenburg. It was the mood of the Homeland. It had changed considerably since the Battalion had marched off so proudly to attack Russia two summers before.

There was something desperate, hectic about it, with the civilians grabbing wildly for their pathetic pleasures, as if death were waiting for them round the very next corner.

He thought suddenly of the woman he had met at a party during his leave in Berlin. At first in her dark, sober clothes, which (though it was forbidden to wear black) indicated she

4. German Officers Mess (transl.)

23

was a war widow. she had seemed like so many German women, living only for the final victory. But after the drink had begun to flow, he had felt an exploratory hand crawl spiderlike up his leg. Twice he pushed it away, thinking that the woman was perhaps unused to drink. But when she began boldly to attempt to undo his flies while the others sang and danced all around them, he knew that he was faced with a determined and experienced woman, eager to have her pleasure. Half an hour later, he was back in her flat, lying naked on the matrimonial bed while she attempted drunkenly to pull off her pants. Sometime during the night she had giggled.

'First one killed in Poland in 39 – Iron Cross Second Class. Second blown to bits in the Ruhr – War Service Cross, First Class. Everything getting bigger and better – whoops, just like this delightful decoration in my hand, eh!'

And the unknown war widow had not been the only one in the two weeks' leave he had spent in Berlin. But it wasn't only the women; it was the black marketeers, the profiteers, the base stallions, hanging on to their safe rear echelon jobs, turning pale at the mere mention of the 'Eastern Front'.

'Hello, Captain von Dodenburg,' a girlish voice broke into his reverie, 'how are you today?'

He turned, startled. It was Karin Schmeer, the only daughter of the local County Leader, staring across at him in her black and white German Maiden uniform.[5] She had eager, bright blue shining eyes, and despite the briefcase full of schoolbooks she was carrying, there were none of the half-promises of the usual schoolgirl about her body. She was tall and well-developed, with good brown muscular legs and full breasts, which threatened to burst out of the thin material of her white silk blouse at any moment.

5. The equivalent of the Hitler Youth organisation for girls. (transl.)

'Oh, it's you, Karin,' he commented unnecessarily. 'On your way back from school?'

'No. We got out at one. I've been to a meeting of the Maidens. We had a talk by that Lesbian – the Area Leader – contraception and the German Woman.' She sniffed prettily. 'Not that she'd know anything about that, would she?'

Von Dodenburg shook his head. 'Where did you hear such talk, Karin, at your age?'

'I'm nearly sixteen. In India I would be a mother now – twice over,' she said firmly and thrust out her big breasts. 'You'd be surprised at what I know, Captain von Dodenburg.' Momentarily she lowered her long eye-lashes and looked up at him through them in what she probably thought was a seductive manner.

Captain von Dodenburg laughed shortly in spite of his mood. 'I'm sure I would, Karin.' He touched his hand casually to the brim of his cap. 'My regards to your father, the County Leader.'

She curtsied gracefully, giving him a quick glimpse of the dark cave of her ample breasts; then she was on her way, swinging her hips from side to side provocatively in a very un-Maidenly manner.

The Commanding Officer of the Wotan Battalion was sitting on a cavalry saddle in the centre of the Casino, swinging his immaculately booted legs angrily and slapping his riding cane against the right one at regular intervals, as von Dodenburg walked in.

'Ah, it's you, von Dodenburg,' he rasped in his unmistakably Prussian voice and screwed his monocle more firmly in his eye above the monstrous beak of a nose which had given him his nickname of 'Vulture'.[6] 'Will you just look at this?'

'What, sir?'

6. *Geier*, his name means 'vulture' in German (transl.)

'This.' With the grace of the regular cavalry officer as he had once been, before he had joined Himmler's Armed SS in order to gain more rapid promotion he swung his leg over the saddle and walked over to von Dodenburg. 'This report from that damn fool of a young spurter who became Lieutenant Schwarz's second-in-command in the Second Company last month. Not only did the craphead take his men to visit the damned cultural anthropological museum in Berlin – without my permission, mark you – but he also had the audacity to send me a full report on the visit.' He slapped the paper with his cane in irritation. 'All about the difference between Jewish and Aryan tibias and similar tommyrot. For all I know they spent their time there in Berlin measuring the length of Yiddish foreskins or some other idiotic rubbish—' he broke off, beside himself with rage.

Captain von Dodenburg bit back his smile just in time. 'Orders from the Reichsführer,' he snapped in his best military fashion, 'the troops are to be instructed in the basic details of Germanic racial superiority.'

'*Racial superiority*,' the Vulture spluttered. 'What the devil does Himmler think we're running here – a school for students still wet behind the spoons – or a military establishment, training soldiers to dodge bullets which make no distiction between a man whose got a damned foreskin a metre long or has had it docked off by some Yid priest armed with a blunt razor blade, eh?'

Captain von Dodenburg thought it wiser to remain silent. The Vulture was unpredictable when he was angry; which was always when the reputation or efficiency of his beloved Wotan was threatened.

The Vulture slapped his cane hard against his boot and strode towards the big French window. He swung round abruptly and levelled the cane at the other officer.

'It all fits in, von Dodenburg. The Battalion's getting soft.

No lice, no hunger, no Popovs shooting at them – and the men go to pieces. Last year at this time they were grubbing in the trenches like a lot of cur dogs for what they could find, and last winter there were some of them who were substituting other kinds of meat for the Old Man ration stuff we got.[7] He looked at von Dodenburg darkly.

The younger officer knew what the CO meant. Last winter when they had been starving in the miserable Kuban marches, there had been three reported cases of cannibalism in the Division when supplies had failed to come up, and Schulze had joked grimly they'd put a couple of kitchen bulls in the 'giddiup soup' now that the horses were running out.[8]

'They're getting soft, von Dodenburg, and I'm not going to have it. By the time this war is over I am going to be a general like my father was before, and those greenbeaks out there are going to get me those stars, whether they like it or not.'

'They're tired, sir,' he said gently.

'Of course they are,' Vulture snapped. 'The whole of Germany's tired. God almighty, we're fighting half the world after all!' He pointed his riding cane at von Dodenburg almost accusingly. 'And that's exactly why we must be hard. The German soldier has to be so hard that he is the match for any two Tommies, Amis or Ivans – and the SS man has to be twice as hard as the ordinary Wehrmacht stubble-hopper. We're the nation's elite, aren't we?' He twisted his ugly face into a cynical grin, and von Dodenburg guessed what he was thinking.

The Armed SS was only a convenient means for him to mount more rapidly up the ladder of promotion; he had no feeling for the sacredness of the National Socialist cause. As

7. Old man=tinned ration meat (transl.)
8. Giddiup soup=horse-meat soup (transl.)

Major Geier often boasted in the Casino: 'Never voted in an election in my life; never read anything since I left school save army reports; and I'm not interested in a thing except those damned general's stars!'

'Do you think then that we'll be sent to the front again soon, sir?' von Dodenburg asked a little hesitantly, not wanting to bring another Geier tirade down upon himself.

'Yes. I got the alert notice from Division this morning. We're on alert stage three.'

'For where?'

The Vulture shrugged. 'I don't know, but I can guess. Eastwards – the bloody Popovs again.' He walked thoughtfully back from the window, his head bent. 'But the men aren't ready for that yet, von Dodenburg. They are not the same men we took to Russia with us the first time. They've not got the same spirit.' Suddenly he looked up and stared at von Dodenburg challengingly. 'But by God, I'm going to give them that same spirit, even if I have to beat it into their hides!' He brought his cane down with a whack on the nearest table. 'Great crap on the Christmas tree, von Dodenburg, when this Battalion marches eastwards again, it's going to be the finest unit in the Army. Now listen, this is what I plan to do when the Tigers arrive . . .'

THREE

There were others among the veterans of SS Assault Battalion Wotan who, like the Vulture and Captain von Dodenburg, were dissatisfied with the state of the Reich. Sergeant Metzger was one. For Lore, his blonde, voluptuous wife, had not received him in the manner he had expected after a year's absence in Russia. On the long three day train trip back to Germany, he had boasted to his cronies of the NCO Corps:

'The second thing I'll do is take my pack off and then I'll tell her she'd better have a good shitty look at the floor because she'll only be seeing the ceiling for the next couple of weeks. Christ, I'm so randy, I can't get up without knocking the mess tins off the table!'

But it hadn't turned out that way. Lore had been obedient enough and they spent his first forty hours in the rented flat's big old-fashioned brass bed with Jesus and his Apostles looking down at their sweaty covorting with saintly, disapproving eyes. Yet somehow she lacked the fiery passion he would have expected from a woman who hadn't had a link slipped to her for twelve months or more, and once when he had reached under the bed for a fresh Parisian[1] and another swig of the good Westphalian beer from the crate he kept there, he had actually caught her yawning, as if with boredom at the whole business.

'There I was,' as he remarked, more than once, to his cronies in the *Ratskeller* cellar bar to which he repaired every afternoon after training, 'pushing my meat into her, the juice pouring off me and my arse going like a Jewish fiddler's elbow – *and she was yawning*, as if all I was doing was scratching her flaming back!'

Sergeant Metzger was not a very intelligent man. Indeed the 'Butcher',[2] as he liked to call himself, was generally regarded as a dumb horned-ox by his comrades of the NCO Corps; but all the same a certain unpleasant suspicion was beginning to grow slowly but surely in his thick, muddled head that all was not well with his blonde plump Lore. As he told his cronies at the *Ratskeller* skat-table in a moment

1. Army slang for a contraceptive (transl.)
2. Metzger='butcher' in German (transl.)

29

of drunken confidence a couple of weeks after they had returned from Russia.

'There's something shitting well wrong there, lads. A big healthy woman like that should be wanting it every night, shouldn't she, especially as she's been so long without a bit. But if I find out that there's been somebody else up her drawers, I'll . . . I'll . . .' He left his threat unuttered, but the quick gesture of his trained butcher's hand, as if he were cutting off something lying very low on the male anatomy, left his red-faced, drunken fellow NCOs in no doubt as to what would happen to the unfortunate man in question, if the Butcher ever caught him.

A couple of times Sergeant Metzger had sneaked home at midday, but he had found Lore alone, pottering around the dusty flat in sleepy boredom. Once he had dropped off the Volkswagen jeep, which came to pick him up every morning, as it had gone round the first corner, doubled back and spent the next couple of hours watching their flat from Hackenschmidt's cigar store across the road. But no one suspicious had entered.

In the end he had been forced to bribe the little sixteen year old Macaroni Mario – all gleaming black greasy hair and shining white teeth – who looked after the apartment house while his parents, both 'volunteer workers' in Paderborn's war factories, were out at work, to keep an eye on Lore and report to him if any men went up to her place.

But although the little spaghetti-eater carried out his task with surprising loyalty and thoroughness for a wop, he had nothing to report, save for once when one of the younger chaplains from the cathedral had come to call in the mistaken belief that Lore was still Catholic.

'You know – a priest,' he had exclaimed excitedly at the bottom of the dark stairs that night when Metzger had come staggering in from the Ratskeller. 'They are all for this, signor.' He made a crude gesture of thrusting his dirty fore-finger through a circle made by the thumb and forefinger of the other hand. 'They no have girls. Always think this.' He had made the obscene gesture once more, looking up at the big German, his dark liquid Italian eyes gleaming fervently.

But Metzger had pushed him roughly to one side. 'No, you shitty spaghetti-eater,' he had growled, 'those blacks don't even know what's for – and even if they did, it'd be the five-fingered widow for them in case they went to hell for doing the other. That's why all the blacks have hair on their palms – too much of the five-fingered widow.' And with that he had staggered on upstairs.

But in the same week that the first of the new Tigers had started arriving at the *Sennelager* railhead from the Stuttgart factories, Sergeant Metzger had, what seemed to him, the first real indication that his suspicions about Lore were justified. As usual Mario received him in the dark hallway and made his report.

'Nothing, signor,' he said with an expressive shrug of his shoulders. 'Nobody come.'

Metzger pointed to his open flies. 'You come perhaps,' he said, mimicking the macaroni's broken German. 'Been visiting the five-fingered widow, Mario, eh?'

The Italian boy coloured hotly and fumbled with his flies, as Metzger passed on his way up the stairs, a broad grin on his red, stupid face. But the grin vanished immediately as Lore called out – even before he had opened the door.

'And wipe those shitty boots of yours on the carpet before you come in! . . . And none of your casual licks, either, do you hear?'

Metzger growled to himself and he gave the door that look which had made many a recruit 'cream his drawers', as

31

he was wont to boast to his drinking cronies; but he did as he was told before entering the little flat.

Lore, plump and blonde, and for some reason highly flushed, sprawled on the sofa in her black artificial silk slip in a manner which showed him she wasn't wearing her pants again – probably, he told himself, because of the heat.

'Well, did you wipe them?' she asked, not looking at him.

'Yes,' he growled. 'I rubbed both my shitty soles off.'

'You don't need to shout – I'm not deaf.' She swung her legs off the back of sofa very carelessly. He caught a glimpse of something very black and hairy against the plump white softness of her thighs.

'Must you always sit around like that?' he snapped, pulling off his pistol belt with a sigh of relief.

'Like what?' she looked at him challengingly.

'Like a five mark whore in a *Reeperbahn*[3] knocking shop,' he answered, tugging at his collar. He poked a sausage-like finger at his tunic with its glittering decorations. 'I'm a senior NCO in the Bodyguard you know, a man who had shed his blood for his Fatherland, for his Folk and Führer – I've got a position to live up to.'

'The only position you can live up to is on yer belly,' she answered contemptuously, 'sticking yer meat in me. That's all you've got in your thick head.'

'Be careful,' he warned threateningly, half raising his hand. He would dearly have liked to have slapped her, but he fancied Lore after supper – and besides it was too hot to quarrel. So he contented himself with dropping into a chair and thrusting out his right leg. 'Dice-beakers,'[4] he ordered.

With a sigh, she straddled her legs over the boot, her plump backside towards him, the damp outline of her cheeks

3. Red-light district in Hamburg (transl.)
4. Army slang for the official issue jackboots (transl.)

presented to his view in what he considered was a very inviting manner. Momentarily he was tempted to let her have a good clap across the arse, but decided against the impulse. Instead he placed his left foot against her buttocks and pushed. With a grunt she pulled off the big boot and dropped it to the carpet. 'The next one,' she said, 'and don't stick your foot so far up my crotch. It hurts.'

He considered letting her have the old Army retort that they wouldn't have found him up there if he hadn't been wearing his size eleven boots, but decided against it.

'Perhaps next time then you'll wear your drawers if it hurts. What if Mario ever came in and saw yer like that just now on the sofa. You know what those shitty spaghetti-eaters are like – one sniff at it and they're walking round stiff-legged.' He sniffed and considered for a moment. 'Well, perhaps not Mario, he's a good lad and he's too young anyway. Too busy with his five against one, more than likely. But his father now, he's different—'

'You're disgusting,' Lore said, and with a grunt tugged off the other boot. 'All you ever think about is that.' She turned round and stared down at him angrily, busily stuffing back one of her ample breasts which had escaped from the confines of her black slip. 'God knows how you ever have time to carry out your duties, when all you've got in your big head is piggeries like that. Mario indeed!' She flung back her long blonde hair. 'Why, he's barely sixteen.'

Metzger pouted. 'Well, when a man's been fighting for his country and away from it for over twelve months, he expects a bit more than—' He never finished his usual complaint, there was the noisy jangle of the flat's bell.

Metzger started up, 'Who in heaven's name is calling at this time of the evening,' he cried angrily. 'What is this place – a fucking transit camp or—'

He broke off suddenly as the door swung open to reveal

the pot-bellied, brown-shirted bulk of County Leader Schmeer himself, collecting box in his fat beringed hand, his sweating face puffed out like the fat backside of the Westphalian pigs he had bred before he become County Leader in 1933.

'Winter Help,' he chortled cheerfully, rattling the box. 'A few pfennigs for the lads at the front!' Then he saw Metzger. 'Oh, it's you Metzger! Didn't know you were home.'

Hastily Lore fled into the bedroom to find a gown while Schmeer's small red eyes followed the swing of her well-rounded buttocks greedily.

'Wouldn't like to have to buy that by the kilo, Metzger, eh?' he commented with a huge knowing wink. 'Christ on a crutch, it's hot isn't it for June!'

Without waiting for an invitation to do so, he dropped into the nearest chair, its ancient springs squeaking in protest at the weight, and pulling out a large brown silk handkerchief wiped the sweat off his gleaming fat face.

'I must have walked at least ten shitty kilometres, rattling this sodding box. Why all those healthy Hitler Youth lads can't do the collecting, I'll never know.' He shrugged good humouredly. 'But I suppose it's up to us Old Fighters[5] to keep the banner flying, what?' He licked his lips significantly. 'Makes you dry though!'

'Would you like a nice cool blond?' Lore said, coming into the room again, tying up her gown which did little to cover those tremendous breasts of hers.

'At my age?' Schmeer said, giving Metzger another of his knowing winks. 'I'm a bit on the old side for that. Leave it to the young uns like Metzger, but I wouldn't mind a beer.'[6]

'Well, you heard the County Leader,' Lore snapped to a

5. Party term for members of the National Socialist Party prior to 1933 (transl.)
6. A pun on the word 'blond', which can stand for a blonde woman and a light beer in German (transl.)

bemused Metzger, who was still trying to recover from the surprise of having the area's most important Party Leader suddenly appear in their shabby rented flat.

'Of course . . . of course,' he stuttered and headed for the kitchen.

'And a little *Korn* wouldn't do any harm, in spite of the heat,' Schmeer called after him. 'A man can't stand on one leg, you know.'

When Metzger came back, he was just in time to see County Leader Schmeer take his big hand off Lore's plump knee. 'The bastard,' he fumed to himself, nearly upsetting the glasses of gin he bore on the tray next to the beer.

Schmeer did not even bat an eyelid. He picked up a bottle of beer, without being asked, flipped open the snap top and raised it in salute to Lore. 'To the ladies – bless 'em,' he chortled. And then to the red-faced fuming Metzger. 'To you comrade, the night's going to be cold!' He took a long draught of the ice-cold beer and belched contentedly. 'Now that's what I call a cultivated glass of beer, Metzger.' He gave a quick sip of his gin to follow it. 'But that's what I expect at the household of Mrs. Sergeant Metzger, isn't it, dear.' He pressed Lore's plump knee once more.

Metzger fought to control his temper. 'How do you mean, County Leader?'

'Well,' Schmeer said expansively, 'I always like to see that the wives of our folk-comrades doing their duty for Folk, Fatherland and Führer at'the front are being looked after. You might say I'm like one of those blacks visiting his parishioners. Every week I did my round while you were in Russia, Metzger, and Mrs Sergeant here always had something waiting for me, didn't you, Lore.'

'Yes, County Leader,' Lore simpered, flattered by so much attention from such an important person.

'I'll give you – *always had something waiting for me, you*

fat pig-breeding bastard!' Metzger cursed to himself. So that was it. It had been the County Leader after all! He'd been the one who had been slipping Lore the link, while he had been slogging it out at the front risking his life for the Greater German Reich!

As he poured the fat County Leader yet another gin, a fake smile covering his broad stupid face, Sergeant Metzger swore undying hatred to the County Leader Adolf Schmeer.

Crimson in the face, County Leader Schmeer was engrossed in slipping the money he had collected from the houses around the great Gothic cathedral into his pocket when he almost bumped into Lieutenant Schwarz, CO of the Wotan's Second Company. Although it was nearly dark now and his head was not too clear after the gins he had drunk at Metzger's flat, he recognised the small SS officer at once.

'Schwarz,' he cried joyfully and stuck out his hand. 'Lieutenant Schwarz of the Bodyguard!'

Schwarz, his hand held protectively on his walking-out dagger, which had been presented to him personally by Reichsführer Himmler, looked at him with his crazy dark eyes, as if the fat Party official might well be some Ivan in disguise.

'Who are you?' he asked in a toneless voice. 'How do you know my name?'

'Schwarz, the nephew of the late General Heydrich.[7] All of us in the Party know about you, Lieutenant. We're not altogether the arsehole of the world here in Paderborn, you know.' He smiled pleasurably, as he saw the young SS officer relax his grip on his dagger. 'The local head of the

7. Reinhard Heydrich, head of the Reich Main Security Office and Deputy Protector of the Occupied Czech state who was assassinated by two Czech para-agents dropped by the British in the summer of 1942.

Gestapo Commissar Gerkin always keeps me informed of any distinguished Party member among our midst – among other things. Besides I knew your late uncle. He was down here in 1938 when we sorted them out. You remember the Crystal Night, don't you? While all those blacks over there in the Cathedral were wringing their hands and wetting their flannel knickers, we really gave the Yids a good working over.'

Slowly Schwarz nodded his head, his face like a crazy death's head in the rays of the blood-red setting sun. He remembered the tremendous revenge the Party had taken on the Jews that night after it had been learned in Britain that the seventeen year old Jew Grynszpan had murdered a German consular official in Paris. Indeed he had taken part in the glorious massacre of Berlin's surviving Yids himself, although he had still worn the short black pants of a Hitler Youth Leader. What a tremendous night that had been – the crash of the stones through the synagogue's windows, the harsh stamp of their boots as they rushed inside and dragged out the screaming fat rabbi to lynch him from the lamppost outside! It had been the turning point in his life – a great purifying experience – which had convinced him he must dedicate himself to the eradication of the Jews and the liquidation of the international Jewish-Bolshevik conspiracy against National Socialist Germany.

But then after he had devoted himself one hundred per cent to that great cause for two years, his uncle – Heydrich – had confessed to him in a moment of drunken rage and self-hatred that his own grandmother was a Jewess, whose first name had been Sarah. What an overwhelming shock that terrible revelation had been! It had ruined his life. He, an SS officer and a member of the Führer's own elite division – the Bodyguard – with a Yid forefather, some greasy hook-nosed Issy, with lice-ridden dirty locks hanging down the side of his evil face—

He broke off his train of thought hurriedly, horrified yet once again at the knowledge that he was living a tremendous lie; for it was a thought that his cracked brain could not tolerate. 'Yes,' Schmeer was chatting away merrily. 'I remember how we got the old Rabbi out – big old fat Hirschbaum. We took his pants off and stood him in a barrel so that everyone could see his little docked Yiddish tail and made him sing the *Horst Wessel Lied* [8]—'

He broke off suddenly and bowed to a black-coated elderly priest who was passing on his way to the Cathedral. 'Good evening, your reverence,' he said, like some town grocer who knows that without the approval of the church, no local would buy his vegetables and he would be broke within the month. 'Very pleasant weather, isn't it, your reverence?'

The elderly priest muttered something inaudible and passed on his way. When he was out of earshot, Schmeer wiped his big fist across his mouth and said apologetically, 'We need the black bastards for a while still, Lieutenant, but when the war's won, there'll be a reckoning with them, believe you me.' His voice rose again. 'I must be off, Schwarz, but I'd be honoured if the nephew of the late General Heydrich would care to come out with me one of these nights when my wife's busy with those ugly sows of the Belief and Beauty group.' [9] He nudged the silent Schwarz and leered at him. 'Even in holy Paderborn, I think I can promise you a bit of something which will make your eyes pop . . . What about next Saturday night?'

Without waiting for the young officer to answer, he said

8. The anthem of the National Socialist Party (transl.)
9. The adult woman organisation of the Nationalist Socialist Party. (transl.)

heartily: 'All right then, that's it. Let's make it next Saturday and you'd better eat your celery salad beforehand, Lieutenant Schwarz, if you know what I mean?' [10]

He leered at Schwarz once more and then he was gone, leaving the crazy young SS officer alone in the centre of the darkening square, a taut little figure his fists clenched in an almost unbearable rage against the dirty trick fate had played him.

But Lieutenant Schwarz was not yet to sample the interesting sexual pleasures that the most catholic bishopric of Paderborn had to offer to the knowledgeable. For with Saturday came also the Royal Air Force in the greatest strength it had ever flown in its thirty year history; Hamburg was burning and SS Assault Battalion was needed.

FOUR

Hamburg was dying. Rapidly, inexorably, it was being eaten up by the greedy, angry flames spreading from the thousands of phosphorous bombs. Even as the Wotan's trucks started to roll across the Elbe bridges they could smell the sweet stench of burning flesh. And before them the whole other bank was aflame. In the cab of the leading truck, his hand shielding his eyes against the orange glare, von Dodenburg could see the 18th century house fronts swaying to and fro like pieces of blazing scenery on a stage. He squirmed round and shouted to Schulze in the back with the men:

'Tell 'em to put their gasmasks on, Sergeant!'

'Sir,' Schulze bellowed over the roar of the flames. 'You heard what the officer said and as soon as we get out, piss

10. It is commonly thought in Germany that celery acts as a sexual stimulant.

on your handkerchiefs and wrap 'em round yer necks. And don't fucking well forget – or when yer shake yer heads, the turnips might well fall off!' But for once the humour was absent from his voice, as he watched his home town vanish before his horrified eyes.

Slowly the convoy of trucks worked its way through the burning streets, the sweat pouring off their drivers' faces as they fought the buildings collapsing on all sides. Twice they came to an abrupt, bone-jarring halt as five hundred pounders hit the earth just in front of the lead truck, exploding in a short thundering roar, followed by a long drawn-out hissing. A moment later the acrid blast swept over them and seemed to drag the air out of their lungs so that they were coughing and choking like old asthmatic men. Finally, however, they reached their destination, the forecourt of the main station, the burning houses on all sides, flooding the cobbled square with a yellowish, white-hot lake as their walls collapsed one after one.

'Everybody out,' von Dodenburg yelled, crunching over the glass-littered cobbles, tripping neatly past the ever-spreading white-hot lake like a ballet dancer. 'Come on, haul ass!'

Hastily the men jumped out of the company's trucks, knowing that if the vehicles remained motionless for more than a couple of minutes their gas tanks would start exploding. Shouting at the top of his voice against the greedy crackle of the flames and the steady crump of the 88 mm flak located in a flak tower some two hundred metres away, von Dodenburg broke his men into details.

A group of panic-stricken amputees in the blue-and-white striped smocks burst into their midst, hopping along on one leg or dragging those by the arms who had lost both legs. Von Dodenburg swallowed hard and fought back the horror which threatened to overcome him, as he saw that some of them were also blind, crawling along on their stumps, screaming for someone to come to their aid.

'Dehn,' he yelled at the corporal standing behind Schulze. 'For God's sake, man, get your detail and help those men into the station's shelter!'

'Sir!'

A woman ran through them screaming in agony, little flames burning on both her naked breasts where phosphorous had buried itself into her skin. Schulze dived for her, but missed. She ran on panic-stricken, the little flames streaming along behind her.

'Holy shit!' Schulze cursed. 'Did you see that poor sow, Captain?'

He nodded, tight-lipped. There was no hope for the woman unless she got herself in water up to her neck; phosphorous would continue burning as long as it was exposed to air or a doctor managed to dig it out with a scalpel.

'Get a detail,' he ordered thickly, fighting back the bile desperately. 'Check they've got their rifles, Schulze. While the rest do the best they can in this mess, we'll have a go at trying to check the looters. You understand me, Schulze?'

'Yessir, you don't need to write it.' Schulze pulled back the flap of his pistol holster and checked that his Walther was ready for action; he knew what the CO meant. Hamburg swarmed with army deserters, black marketeers and foreign workers who made a business of looting immediately after the raids, coming out of their dirty holes like so many longtails searching alley trashcans for carrion.

A few moments later they set off, marching carefully down the centre of the great avenue that led from the Alster to the station, with von Dodenburg, Schmeisser machine pistol cradled in his arm in the lead, and Schulze, Walther held in his hamlike fist, bringing up the rear.

They passed a city fire engine. Its motor was still running.

41

But the firemen had suffocated in the baking heat. Now they sat in their prescribed positions along both sides of the ladder, the clothes burnt off them, naked save for their boots and helmets.

'At the double!' von Dodenburg yelled.

Readily the file broke into a run, their heavy boots crunching over shattered slates and broken glass, not daring to glance at the dead men on the engine. A few seconds later the vehicle's gas tank exploded and the firemen disappeared in a vicious ball of ugly red and yellow flames.

They came closer to the city's pride – the internal lake called the Alster. In the ruddy glare of the burning buildings on the other side, they could see the phosphorous victims paddling about everywhere, desperately trying to keep their burnt bodies submerged. Weakening visibly by the effort, their cries for help seemed like an age-old prayer in which they no longer believed.

But the elderly policemen piling up the victims from the burning hotel nearby had no time for them. A few were still alive, but most were charred by the searing flames and shrivelled up to the size of black pigmies, and the policemen stacked them as if they were logs of wood.

'Human child . . . oh, you holy human child!', Schulze suddenly gasped with horror, 'look at that!'

The patrol swung round. On the other side of the road, the line of trees which bordered it had been stripped bare of their leaves by the blast, with here and there a thick branch snapped off as if it had been a matchstick. But it was not the damage which had caused Schulze's horrified cry. It was the naked babies, blown among the branches from the nearby nursery, hanging there dead like overripe fruit.

Von Dodenburg swung his head back nauseated, choking back the bitter bile. He marched on, feeling he himself was a dead man among thousands of dead.

The 88s had stopped firing from the flak tower somewhere over by Dammtor station. To the north the first of the city's sirens started sounding the thin strains of the 'all clear'. The Tommies were going, their murderous assault on the city completed, leaving it now to its death throes. They marched by the burning *Hotel Vier Jahreszeiten* towards the *Jungfernstieg*, the port's great shopping centre.

'Keep your eyes peeled,' von Dodenburg forced himself to order. 'The rats will be coming out, now they're safe.'

The pale-faced troopers gripped their weapons more firmly, their shadows thrown into monstrous trembling relief by the flames. But the *Jungfernstieg* and its stores were a burning rain; and the civilians crowding it were not looters, but panic-stricken Hamburgers fleeing the dying city, wet rags wrapped round their faces, the steam rising from their dampened clothes. Everywhere burning bodies lay sprawled out in the gutters and a little white dog kept running in front of their feet, yelping crazily, as if it were seeking some dead master. Wordlessly Schulze raised his Walther and shot it neatly through the head. It sank down almost gratefully and died on the spot.

They plodded on through the refugees and the handful of city officials trying to organise them, without success. Once they stopped a figure running out of a burning house, a sack clutched in his hands. But the elderly man was not looting. He was the owner of the place who had risked his life to rush in and fetch out a bundle of Field Post letters from his son who had vanished at Stalingrad.

'But it's all I've got now, all I've got . . .' he kept repeating as they let him go to join the stream of refugees.

A little later they came across a white-haired old woman who could have been anyone's grandmother; save that she was completely naked and had a dead baby clutched to her ancient leathern dug, which had not given milk these fifty

43

years, urging it to drink with the clucking noises nursing mothers make to encourage their infants. She would not move, nor would she answer their shouted questions and in the end they were forced to leave her, squatting on the curb, the dead child clutched to her skinny ancient body, as the sea of flame swept ever closer.

Five minutes later they were pressed into service to keep back a crowd of screaming frantic civilians while an officer in the combat engineers and a handful of men prepared to blow up an underground air raid shelter to make a fire break which might prevent the fire storm from spreading.

'But there are still women and children in there!' a hysterical middle-aged woman, whose hair had been burned away to a military crop, kept screaming at the harassed young officer. 'I know, I tell you! I just heard them shouting for help before you came . . . You must listen – there are children down there!'

But the young officer ignored her as he fumbled frantically with the detonator, and she relapsed into a heart-broken sobbing.

'If there were a God, He wouldn't allow this to happen – I know He wouldn't!' a woman next to her said angrily.

'Leave God out of this,' an old man, who looked like a former NCO in the old Imperial Army, snapped sharply. 'God doesn't make war – men do!'

With a grunt the young engineer officer pressed the detonator plunger. There was a thick throaty muffled crump, a vicious stab of ugly yellow flame shot into the red air and what was left of the building above the underground air-raid shelter collapsed on top of it, sealing it off for good, leaving its occupants to die slowly from lack of oxygen.

Grimly they plodded on, leaving behind them the sobbing women.

It was just before they reached the main station once again that they bumped into the two elderly policemen leading the seven RAF prisoners burdened with their parachutes and sweating heavily in their thick fur-lined flying overalls.

'Tommies?' von Dodenburg snapped in a strange voice, stopping the patrol.

The bigger of the two city policemen, his fat chest covered with World War One decorations, snapped to attention, his eyes warily taking in the SS runes.

'Yes, Captain. They came down just behind the Fish Market. We're taking them to the central police station. The Army can collect them there—'

'You're shitting well not!' Schulze burst in savagely, his teeth bared like those of some wild animal.

'*Schulze!*' barked von Dodenburg.

But the big Hamburger was beyond listening. He stared at the RAF men, a couple of them who were injured, his eyes glittering crazily.

'Those sodding bastards don't deserve to sit out the rest of the war in some shitty POW camp, living off their Red Cross parcels. Not when they've done this!' He swung his big hand, with the pistol in it, around at the fiery burning background. 'They're not soldiers – *they're cold-blooded killers!*'

'Now careful, Sergeant,' the bigger cop said. 'You can't talk like that. We've got our orders—'

'Piss up your sleeve,' Schulze swung round to von Dodenburg. 'What do you say, sir? Are we going to let the Tommy bastards get away with this? Isn't it our duty to punish them – here and now?'

Captain von Dodenburg bit his lip. He thought of the blind amputees crawling on their stumps to the safety of the station, the naked old crone with her dead infant, the bodies

45

hanging in the trees; then he looked at the Tommies staring at the armed SS men uncomprehendingly.

'Put them against that wall,' he snapped suddenly.

'Hey, you can't do that,' the bigger cop said angrily.

'Hold yer trap and give your arse a chance,' Schulze roared, pushing him aside as he tried to place his fat body in front of his prisoners.

The other one tried to bring up his pistol, but one of the troopers brought his rifle butt down sharply onto his arm. He howled with sudden pain and his pistol dropped to the littered cobbles with a clatter of metal.

'What's going on here?' cried a burly Tommy with a great curling moustache stained red with the blood running down the side of his face, in broken German. 'We're prisoners of—' He broke off suddenly. The looks on the sweating faces of the young SS troopers told him all he wanted to know.

A red-haired Tommy, who looked all of seventeen, standing next to him asked him something in alarm. But the one who spoke German shook his head and put out his hand to steady him. To no effect. The red-haired kid dropped on his knees and raising his hands in the traditional posture of supplication, he babbled something in English. His words ended in a shriek of pain, as one of the troopers, beside himself with rage at what he had seen that night, kicked him squarely in the mouth.

Thereafter the RAF men remained silent. Wordlessly they allowed themselves to be lined up against the nearest wall, tugging the sobbing red-haired youth with them. They tried to raise him to his feet. But failed. So they stood there, their faces ruddy and sweaty against the flames, their eyes blank of fear as hate – blank of any emotion at all.

Von Dodenburg lined his men up to face them. Without an order, they raised their rifles. The Captain brought up

46

his Schmeisser, while the two elderly cops looked on in horrified impotence. One word of protest from them and they knew they would join the RAF men; they were both veterans of the trenches in the First War. They'd seen men like these, shocked out of their minds by the horrors of war before, and knew there was no stopping them now.

For a moment nothing happened. The Tommies about to die stared numbly at their killers. There was no sound save the steady crackle of the flames and the thick sobbing of the boy with the ruined mouth.

'*Fire!*' von Dodenburg screamed suddenly. Almost without knowing he pressed the trigger of his machine pistol. It crackled into life at his side. At such close range, his burst ripped the face off the Tommy with the big moustache, transforming it into a shapeless red pulp. Then the others joined in the murder of the RAF prisoners.

It was all over in a matter of seconds. For a moment they stood there, listening to the heavy echoing silence, while the two elderly cops stared at them open-mouthed. Before them the smoking bodies sprawled out now in the careless, abandoned postures of the violently done-to-death. The bigger of the two policemen raised his thick forefinger and pointed it accusingly at von Dodenburg. '*You . . . you*,' he began, but no other words came.

Von Dodenburg swallowed. His mouth was abruptly terribly dry. 'Follow me,' he whispered hoarsely.

Obediently they turned and followed him towards the station, stumbling through the smoking debris of a dying Hamburg, their chests heaving violently as if they had just run a great race. Behind them the two elderly cops did not move, the bigger one his thick forefinger still pointing as if in eternal accusation.

47

The order came from the Berlin Headquarters of the Armed
SS. It read:

'In view of the exceedingly efficient manner in which the
SS Assault Battalion Wotan recently executed its arduous
mission during the English air gangsters' terror attack on
the Free Hansa City of Hamburg, the Reichsführer SS takes
pleasure in granting the Battalion a three day stand down
from its training schedule. This order is to take effect immediately.'

Heil Hitler!

(signed) Himmler.

And even the Vulture dare not disobey the order from the
ex-chicken farmer who was now the most feared man in
Europe. Reluctantly he granted the whole Battalion three
days' local leave, and cursed the Reichsführer SS to high
heaven as he signed the order which Captain von Dodenburg
set before him.

But the men of Wotan took no pleasure in this surprise
respite from the dreary round of training. Those three terrible days in the dying Hamburg, which they'd ended by
bulldozing the great heaps of dead into mass graves, had
taken their toll. And there was not one of them who wanted
to do anything else but blot out the ghastly memories of that
place, with its 40,000 dead within five hours, by means of
massive doses of alcohol.

Even the seventeen-year-old 'greenbeaks', who had never
touched a glass of beer before they had been rushed to Ham-

burg, went out that first day and began to drink themselves into insensibility with dogged sullen determination, pouring the *Korn* and *Pils* into themselves in the dark little bars all over the provincial city, oblivious to the severe looks of the elderly gentlemen sitting round their *stammtische* [1] playing skat.

Sergeant Schulze hardly waited for County Leader Schmeer to leave the house with his daughter before he blundered in through the kitchen door, his cap on the back of his head, his tunic ripped open and his big face flushed a sullen red.

Mrs Schmeer, ten years younger than her husband, but just as fat, was standing at the oven watching Heidi frying his favourite Schnitzel and potatoes.

'Won't be long my big hero,' she chirped, her face flushed with cooking. 'I want to get it just right for you.'

Heidi of the big knockers kept her head bent pretending she wasn't aware of the big NCO's presence. Schulze, already very drunk from the Korn he had been pouring down his throat all afternoon, was in no mood for Frau Schmeer or her Schnitzel. What he wanted this day was oblivion. With an angry swipe of his big hand, he sent the frying pan flying.

'Stick yer Schnitzel up your fat arse,' he snarled drunkenly, nearly falling over, 'piss off into the cellar and get me a bottle of Schnaps – *two bottles!*'

Heidi bent down to pick up the meat, but he caught her by the blouse to stop her. It ripped badly. Her massive breasts, unrestrained by any bra, tumbled out. She screamed and tried to cover them with her hands.

'Get those hands away,' he cried, 'I want to see yer tits!'

'But my big hero,' Mrs Schmeer protested, too concerned that he might not give her what she needed in bed that

1. Roughly 'regular tables', a feature of German pubs which are reserved for the same regular guests by means of the *Stammtisch* sign (transl.)

evening to be angry about the Schnitzel. 'You can't do—'

'Have you got cloth ears – have you been eating big beans?' he bellowed. Can't you hear me? I said – piss off into the cellar and get me something to drink. I'm going upstairs with Heidi and I want something to drink before I push it in her . . . Now fetch that flaming bottle of booze, will you?'

'But she's my maid. You can't—'

'*Fetch it!*' Schulze raised his big fist threateningly and she fled in alarm, while the big Sergeant stamped unsteadily upstairs, dragging the screaming, half-naked maid with him.

But when Frau Schmeer timorously knocked on the maid's door and crept in, holding the tray as if she were ready to drop it and run at any moment, Schulze's rage had fled. Heidi was standing in the centre of the room, her enormous breasts uncovered staring down puzzled at a Schulze who lay on his stomach on the bed, sobbing hopelessly, beating the bed every now and again with his big fist and crying in his utter despair: 'Why did it shitting well have to happen . . . oh, why?'

There were many others of the Wotan Battalion who could not answer that overwhelming question. Captain von Dodenburg was one. He staggered blindly through the Cathedral city's evening streets, while Schwarz, just as drunk, marched blankly at his side. Everywhere there were drunken SS men, crowding the straight-laced, shocked civilians off the pavements, forgetting to salute the officers and NCOs (who were just as intoxicated), urinating against house walls to the horror of the prudish Catholic housewives.

Von Dodenburg was vaguely aware that they were from the Wotan and that their behaviour this day had ruined the Battalion's reputation for discipline and order in Paderborn. But he did not care. All he could see in his mind's eye was the dead babies hanging in the stripped trees like monstrous human fruit.

'I don't care, I don't care, Schwarz,' he mumbled drunkenly and nearly tripped. Gravely Schwarz steadied him and nodded his crazy head, muttering something unintelligible.

They stumbled on. Then a voice interrupted their confused reverie as they turned into the central square. 'Gentlemen – gentlemen, how glad I am to see you.' A hand caught hold of von Dodenburg's arm and pulled him to a stop.

With a great effort of will, von Dodenburg turned slowly. A blurred brown outline filled his vision. He shook his head stupidly to bring it into focus. A piglike shining Westphalian face above a brown SA uniform appeared with next to it a blonde head of hair, rolled into little 'snails' over the ears, supported by a well-filled German Maiden uniform.

'Captain von Dodenburg – Lieutenant Schwarz,' the pig face said jovially.

'Don't know you,' von Dodenburg said thickly, slurring his words. 'Shit of,' he threw off the restraining hand and staggered on.

'Grab hold of him, Karin, for Christ's sake,' Schmeer snapped to his daughter, while he hung on to Schwarz. 'He's going to get himself in trouble with the chaindogs[2] if they catch him in that state.'

'At your service,' Karin answered cheekily. 'You've always been good at giving orders, County Leader.'

All the same she ran quickly after von Dodenburg while her father beamed at Schwarz and said: 'I think one more beer, Lieutenant, and then I feel I should show you some of those little pleasures that I promised you the last time we me. What do you say, Lieutenant Schwarz?'

2. Army MPs, named after the silver chain plates they wore round their necks while on duty (transl.)

Schwarz belched and nodded his crazy head. 'Beer . . . pleasures,' he mumbled.

Schmeer waited till his daughter had caught up with the other officer and thrust her arm under his, steadying him somewhat as he blundered his way through a crocodile of giggling young chaplains, before turning back to Schwarz again.

'All right, Lieutenant, now we've got rid of her, I think we can go.'

Obediently Schwarz allowed himself to be led into the dark cobbled, grass-overgrown streets, which smelled of ancient lecheries and unwashed bodies while the heavy frowning facade of the great Gothic cathedral stared down at them in silent reproach.

Her firm arms ringed his neck and she thrust her tongue between his open lips. He smelled of beer, but she didn't care. Her whole body was trembling with desire, and she could feel her nipples growing erect. Savagely she thrust her soft stomach into his. But there was no stirring there as yet.

'Shit – shit on the Christmas Tree,' she cursed.

But he didn't seem to hear. He just stood there swaying, as if he was concentrating his whole energy on remaining erect. Swiftly she released her hold and when she was sure he would not fall back onto her bed, surveyed by the Führer's scowling face, she pulled the buttons of her skirt and let it fall. Impatiently she ripped off her blouse, watching him all the time. But her sudden nakedness did not seem to affect him.

For a moment she hesitated. Almost unconsciously she ran her hands over her big breasts and gently squeezed the now erect nipples. Then she tugged at her pants, white, simple and the kind schoolgirls wore. Provocatively she

52

thrust out the black thatch at his belly. But still he did not react.

'Come on you big, handsome, aristocratic bastard,' she hissed, 'get it up. *I want it!*'

She placed the elegant hands she had so admired the first time she had met the young officer onto her breasts, hard and swollen with desire now.

'But you're only sixteen,' he said thickly, speaking for the first time since she had sneaked him up the stairs to her own bedroom.

She laughed cynically. 'What difference does it make?' She thrust her belly against him and ran her hot little tongue into his ear momentarily. 'Sixteen or sixty – it's just the same, save it's tighter.'

With a practised hand she ripped open his flies like a factory worker pulling a lever and thrust her hands into the dark cave of his field-grey breeches and ran her greedy fingers over what she found there.

Suddenly, as if a dam had burst, it worked. She could feel it grow by the instant. Unable to control the trembling of her legs, she drew him carefully to the bed, still greedily holding on to it. She lowered herself and spread her legs.

'It'll hurt,' he said thickly, but it was desire not drink which was distorting his speech now.

'What?'

'This.' He touched the delightful thing with his elegant hand. 'If you're a virgin.'

She nearly laughed in his handsome face. But she did not want to hurt him. 'Yes, of course,' she said and then sotto voce. 'But not this year, Captain von Dodenburg, sir.'

Swiftly she raised her long slim brown legs high in the air to make a cradle for his hard young muscular body. 'I think it's time to climb aboard, Captain von Dodenburg,' she whispered hoarsely, her lips suddenly very dry and her heart pounding almost unbearably.

As he descended upon her eagerly, the last thing she caught sight of was the Führer's face staring down at her in black disapproval of such un-Maidenly conduct. Then she gasped with pleasure and forgot everything else.

The whores were dark, flashy, exotic and somehow un-German. But their accents were pure harsh East Westphalian. And they were afraid of his uniform with its silver SS runes, even Schwarz's befuddled drunken brain could recognise that.

But the pot-bellied County Leader was well known there. He clapped the tired-looking Madam across her fat, black-silk buttocks and cried joyfully. 'No beer tonight, Rachel. In honour of my young friend here, I think we'll have champus!'

'Champus!' the dark-eyed whores cried in faked enthusiasm.

'You're in for five hundred marks already this month, County Leader,' the middle-aged Madam with dyed hair said wearily, as if she had made the same statement many times before and knew she were wasting her breath.

'I know my beautiful Rachel,' Schmeer chortled. 'But if the worst comes to the worst, the Reichsführer SS will solve that problem for me, won't he?' He looked at her cunningly for a moment with his small piggish eyes and made a strange spiralling gesture with his fat forefinger like smoke going up a chimney. The Madam blanched.

'All right, County Leader, champus it'll be.' Hastily she waddled away to fetch the champagne.

Schmeer beamed and nudged Schwarz. 'That's the way to treat 'em. Sugar and the whip as the Führer used to say in the old days – that gets 'em working.'

Schwarze nodded blindly and slumped down in the nearest armchair. Immediately one of the dark-haired whores, her sallow cheeks heavy with rouge, her heavy body covered in a black silk petticoat plumped herself on his lap and began to run her hands over his body in routine passion.

The cheap sweet French champagne began to flow. The girls relaxed. As the alcohol started to have its effect, they became more and more abandoned. Giggling hysterically a couple of them dipped a befuddled Schwarz's middle finger into a glass of champagne and maintained loudly that the distorted reflection would indicate the size of his organ.

A red-faced Schmeer joined in the fun. He allowed the Madam and another whore – a skinny girl clad only in a black corset and silk stockings – to take off his brown boots and breeches, laughing uproariously as they tugged hard at the tight breeches and nearly fell over when they slipped back abruptly.

As two of the others danced obscenely, cheek to cheek, their hands clasped round each other's buttocks like apache dancers, the Madam and the skinny whore occupied themselves with Schmeer's flaccid organ dangling below an enormous white hairless belly, while the County Leader laughed with uncontrollable laughter at the antics of the other two girls.

The room in the cheap brothel began to revolve around Schwarz. The girls' drunken giggles and the pleasure grunts made by a red-faced County Leader grew and receded like the ebb and flow of waves. Vaguely he was aware of the dark whore on his lap nuzzling her wet sensual lips against his face. The grunts grew ever louder; the giggles more shrill; the waves receded ever further. Then suddenly he was gone and a great darkness descended before his eyes.

He came to in a dirty rumpled bed with the whore who

55

had sat on his lap bending over him, her face strained and tired, yet somehow concerned, as she wiped his face with cold water in almost a motherly fashion.

'You all right, Lieutenant?' she asked.

His black eyes stared up at her blankly and then swept around the grubby little bedroom with the red marks of squashed bedbugs on the unpainted walls and patched tears in the blackout curtains made of dyed blankets. His eyes came to an abrupt halt. A coat was hanging from a bent nail behind the door. It was shabby and worn, just like the room. But it wasn't its shabbiness which caught Schwarz's attention. It was the yellow emblem sewn prominently on its left breast.

Her weary eyes followed the direction of his gaze. '*Yours?*' he breathed, the sight shocking a reaction even out of his befuddled crazy brain.

She nodded slowly.

'But it's the Jewish Star!'

'I know – the Star of David . . . I'm Jewish, Lieutenant.'

'*Jewish?*' he echoed in horror. 'Half?'

'No,' she shook her head firmly. 'Full. Both my parents were orthodox.' She shrugged carelessly. 'Not me, though. And then this—' she left the sentence unfinished and stared down at him unconcerned, as if there were nothing strange about a full Jewess confessing her crime to an SS officer in the year 1943.

'But . . . how . . ?' He stuttered horrified, trying to find words to express his outrage.

'How?' she laughed cynically. 'Easy. There are many who come here especially, like County Leader Schmeer. We're all Jewish here, and they know it. It has a particular sexual appeal for them. Party officials, SS men, officers like you. They can insult us. They can beat us. They can try out their little perversions – like Schmeer – and there is an extra pleasure in it for them because we are Jewish. And after all, it's better than the camps, you know?' She raised her tired voice and repeated the fixed tenet of the Party: 'Jews are the cancer of society and must be removed with surgical ruthlessness!' She grinned bitterly and slumped down on the sagging bug-ridden bed next to him.

He recoiled. 'Don't touch me Jewess,' he cried. *'Don't!'* · Her hands caressed his body and he could feel the horror of her dirty Jewish fingers fumbling with his clothes.

'Why not, my little SS man?' she whispered. 'Men are men, aren't they – whether they're Aryan or Jewish?' Now she had opened his flies and was fondling him. 'Don't fight me, let me love you,' she urged with professional hoarseness. 'Let me show you we are no different. We have hearts and bodies and c—'

He summoned up all his strength, and pushed. 'Let me go,' he screamed in a broken voice. 'For God's sake, let me go – please Jewess. *Please!'*

As she fell to one side in surprise, he sprang drunkenly from the bed and ran to the door in a blind panic. Flinging it open, he slipped and fell down the narrow dark stairs. But he didn't seem to feel the pain in his haste to get away from the Jewish whore. He blundered into the dusky-red reception room, nearly knocking over the skinny whore in black stockings who was bent busily over Schmeer's hairless pot-belly.

'Jesus, Mary, Joseph!' he cursed angrily, starting up out of his ecstasy, 'what in the hell's name has got into you, Schwarz?'

But the SS officer was already fumbling frantically with the outside door. He could not get it open. In his haste he kicked it savagely. It flew open and he blundered out into the night. Seconds later he was leaning against the wall in the back alley, which stank of cabbage and cat's piss, retching miserably, as if he would never stop again. At his side, a worried Schmeer, a tablecloth hurriedly wrapped around his naked belly, and the Jewish whore, the tell-tale coat slung over her bare shoulders, stared at him in awed bewilderment.

Finally they managed to persuade him to come inside again, after the whore had used Schmeer's tablecloth to clean his lips of the vomit. His thin shoulders heaving as if he were sobbing violently, though his crazy face was blank of tears or any other expression of emotion, he allowed himself to be led into the brothel. The door closed behind the strange little group once more.

As it did so, Metzger got up unsteadily from behind the ashcans where he had hidden as soon as he had recognised Lieutenant Schwarz. He wiped the rotting vegetables off his knees and swayed once more with the load of schnapps and beer he had taken aboard at the *Ratskeller* that evening. His eyes gleamed with triumph, for in spite of his drunkenness he had not failed to spot that yellow star the whore had worn. She was a Yid and she had been with County Leader shitty Schmeer who had been slipping his Lore a link while he had been away at the front fighting for Folk, Fatherland and Führer.

'Now you fat bastard of a golden pheasant,' [3] he breathed triumphantly at the closed door, 'I've got you, got you right by your bloody eggs!' He tried to adjust his cap to the correct military angle and failed miserably. But he didn't care. As he emerged from the stinking alley into the blacked-out square, he thrust out his big chest and marched towards his flat, as if he were in charge of the guard at the Führer's Headquarters itself, his little red eyes gleaming vindicatively. County Leader Schmeer was as good as dead already.

3. Contemptuous army name for the rear line Party officials, due to their habit of wearing a lot of gold braid (transl.)

SIX

'You're a lot of wet tails – soft wet tails, full of piss and fried potatoes!' the Vulture rasped in his high-pitched Prussian voice, staring down at them from the deck of the new Tiger, the sweat streaming down his monstrous nose.

The 800 odd young men of Wotan, the elite of the National Socialist state, stared up at him wordlessly, their open sun-burned faces serious and worried.

'You've been too long in the Homeland,' the Vulture continued. 'Been too busy filling your guts. Too busy pushing an easy ball. You forget that we are fighting a war of survival and that at this very moment, good men – better men than you – are dying by their hundreds in the East so that you parasites can live an easy life here in Westphalia. But it's going to stop, I can tell you that. Great crap on the Christmas Tree, it's going to stop!' He brought his riding cane down hard against the side of his boot and one or two of the young men in the front rank jumped startled. 'Even if I have to kill every single one of you greenbeaks in the process!'

The Vulture swung his angry burning eyes around their faces as they stood there in the white hot June afternoon, grouped around the first squadron of Tigers which had been delivered from the railhead that very morning.

'You men must learn that we do not play games in SS Assault Battalion Wotan. We are the Führer's elite – the Führer's Fire Brigade, I believe, is the term that is used in headquarters. But at the moment you men – thin streaks of piss that you are – couldn't put out a grassfire.' He looked down at them scornfully. 'Because you're soft. *Soft*, do you understand? *Soft as shit!* Today the kid gloves are finally off, I can promise you that. Today you are going to learn what it means to have the honour of serving in the Führer's Fire Brigade.'

He drew a deep breath and made a visible effort to control himself, though as an admiring von Dodenburg, watching his CO's tremendous performance, knew the Vulture was in complete charge of his faculties. His rage was deliberate and artificial, meant to sting the young recruits to the Battalion into a reaction – any reaction.

'Behind me,' he snapped, 'you will be able to see a thirty seven millimetre anti-tank gun. Not a very powerful weapon admittedly, but one which can give you a nice little headache at close range if it hits you.' He smiled thinly at his own humour, but there was no answering gleam in his cold eyes.

'Under me, there is a metal steed that can be stopped by no known anti-tank canon, if it is handled correctly.' He kicked the Tiger's great turret with his gleaming spurred riding boot which he always wore although he had left the cavalry in 1937. 'The glacis plate[1] of the Tiger cannot be penetrated by a thirty-seven millimetre shell even at a range of two hundred metres. Of course it's unpleasant to hear the shells knocking at your front door at such short range,' he grinned down at their earnest young faces cynically. 'But then there are those who cream their drawers when a window rattles on a dark night.'

He raised his voice. 'Now today it is my intention to start making men out of you greenbeaks. Every tank crew in the battalion will drive down the course which has been staked out behind you at a speed of twenty kilometres an hour. As soon as your vehicle reaches the green marker, Lieutenant Schwarz and Captain von Dodenburg manning the 37 mm

1. The steep front plate of the tank, usually the most heavily armoured part of any armoured fighting vehicle (transl.)

will open fire.' He paused for the expected gasp of surprise and got it.

The Vulture grinned thinly and continued. 'The 37 will fire three shells. When your vehicle reaches the white marker here – at two hundred metres range – the tank commander will break right and drive off the range. One word of warning, however. If any one of you decides to break off before he reaches that white marker, I shall order Lieutenant Schwarz and Captain von Dodenburg to open fire at the vehicle's flank. And let there be no doubt about it – at that range a 37 mm can penetrate even the Tiger. Someone will get more than creamed skivvies – he'll get a very bloody nose.'

He let his words sink in for a moment; then he blew his whistle. At the far end of the range, Schulze's driver started up his engine with a roar. The monstrous sixty ton Tiger with its great hooded overhanging 88 mm cannon lumbered forward. The men of the Wotan scattered, while Schwarz and von Dodenburg ran towards the anti-tank gun.

'*Fire!*' the Vulture yelled, as Schulze's tank crossed the start-line.

At that range Schwarz could not miss. The white tracer hissed flatly across the range, striking the centre of the Tiger's glacis plate. Momentarily the metal glowed a dull red. Then the shell went soaring upwards into the deep blue sky like a cheap penny rocket. Hastily von Dodenburg reloaded, the sweat pouring down his face. Schwarz snatched the firing lever again. A blast of hot air hit von Dodenburg in the face like a flabby fist. He gasped, automatically opening his mouth to prevent his eardrums from being burst, and stared over the shield.

The shell smacked home with a great hollow clang of metal striking metal. The Tiger rocked slightly. But again the

37 mm shell went soaring off like a golfball, leaving a bright new silver scar on the glacis plate.

Just before Schulze's Tiger reached the white marker, Schwarz fired for the last time. Sparks flew from the front of the tank and it reared up on its hind sprockets like a bucking horse; then Schulze's Tiger was swivelling round crazily, throwing up a huge cloud of dust.

'Three direct hits,' the Vulture rasped through his megaphone, staring down at the awed, round-eyed troopers, 'and not one penetration. That, as even your thick heads can undoubtedly perceive, makes the Tiger a war-winning weapon. Now—'

'But, sir,' Horten, Schwarz's second-in-command, broke in. 'Can we afford to allow our new vehicles to be damaged in an exercise like this? Surely the demonstration we have just seen should suffice to convince us of the value of this weapon made by our folk-comrades?'

The Vulture looked down at the pale-faced young second lieutenant who had just joined the Battalion from the Bad Toelz Officer School the month before, as if he had just popped up from the earth.

'My dear Horten,' he rasped. 'Your folk-comrades, as you call them, are the scum of Europe, bribed or beaten to come to Germany to work in our industries. Before I would trust my life to the workmanship of some Polack or spaghetti-eater, I would want to see how the vehicle they have produced stands up to fire. Unfortunately in actual battle, my dear Horten, as you will undoubtedly find out, the Popovs don't allow one to settle down in the middle of the fight and make up for the deficiencies – or sabotage, if you like – of your folk-comrades.'

There was some sniggering in the rear ranks of the Battalion and Horten's pale face flushed red with embarrassment. He opened his mouth to say something else, but the Vulture didn't give him a chance.

'Mount up!' he yelled through the megaphone. 'Every crew to its vehicle!'

Hastily the SS men broke ranks and doubled across the uneven range towards the waiting steel monsters. The next instant the still afternoon was broken by the roar of engine after engine bursting into powerful life. One after the other the raw crews rattled down the range to face up to their frightening baptism of fire. Time and time again there was the angry whang of metal striking metal. Young troopers staggered out of the vehicles, white-faced and shocked. Others did not manage to clamber out of the turrets, but vomited where they stood, their heads ringing still with the impact of the 37 mm shells at such close range.

But the Vulture would not allow any let-up. He urged ever fresh crews into the Tigers, chivvying the young soldiers with his cynical rasping voice, while von Dodenburg sweated over the breech of the red-hot anti-tank gun, the pile of gleaming smoking shell cases mounting ever higher behind him.

And then it happened. A frightened tank commander ordered his Tiger to break away after the second shell had jarred his tank from side to side. The Vulture, his eyes gleaming angrily, did not hesitate.

'Schwarz,' he yelled above the roar of the Tiger's great engines. 'Let him have it to the right of the turret mount!'

Schwarz, his eye glued to the rubber eye-piece, took a quick aim. The next instant he fired. The 37 mm canon jerked wildly, its trails starting up from the dusty ground. But no one had eyes for the anti-tank gun. Their gaze was fixed on the Tiger.

Schwarz's shell caught the tank exactly at its weak spot – the turret ring. Angry red sparks flew up from the thin metal. It heaved back on its sprockets like a live thing. A sharp spike of ugly yellow flame stabbed out of its engine cowling. There was a gasp of horror from the spectators.

'Bale out . . . for Chrissake – *bale out*!' von Dodenburg yelled wildly. He dropped the shell he was holding and doubled forward. His move broke the spell. Suddenly they were all running towards the fiercely burning Tiger from which dark shapes were now tumbling blindly, screaming in agonized pain.

But their aid came too late for the tank commander who had been too scared to face up to that last shell. He lay dead on the scorched grass, angry blue flames still licking his blackened body.

Carelessly the Vulture turned the body over with his elegantly booted foot, and stared down at the black-charred face in bored curiosity. 'As I thought,' rasped. 'Friend Horten of the anthropological studies.' He looked at von Dodenburg cynically and then removing his polished riding boot allowed the body to fall on its first-burst stomach again. 'Well, now he knows that the length of your foreskin is no indication of your bravery, what, von Dodenburg!'

The Vulture slapped his cane against his boot. 'All right, you wet tails,' he roared at the wide-eyed young soldiers crowding in on all sides to get a glimpse at the dead officer sprawled out extravagantly in the blackened grass. 'So you've seen your first stiff. Good. Now then, let's get on with the exercise, yes . . .'

Time was running out. That was clear even to the rawest recruit of SS Assault Battalion Wotan. Every day the Vulture stepped up the pressure – platoon-strength attack, company-attack, battalion-attack; tank support attack with infantry; night attacks; partisan defence attacks. Hour after hour from six in the morning until late at night when the red ball of the June sun finally sank below the flat Westphalian horizon and the recruits could stagger off blindly to their bunks, the veteran NCOs and officers of the old Wotan poured the knowledge of four years of war into the green-beaks' ears.

'At night when the Ivan T-34s come at yer, don't wet yer knickers, let them have a couple of star shells straight to the turret. That'll blind the Ivan gunner long enough for even duds like you to get in the first shot . . .'

'Wait till the T-34s breast the rise. Then you've got 'em by the short, black and curlies. Their big old guts – with no armour – will be showing. *Zap!* Yer let 'em have one there, just as if yer slipping yer girl friend a quick link. That is – those of you who like girls . . .'

'Their tank radio communication is crap – virtually non-existent. The Ivans can't build radios because they've got six shitty fingers on each dirty hand. So what happens when they try to launch a concentrated attack? I'll tell you, wet tails. They get out little flags and start signalling to each other like a lot of shitty boy scouts. What do you do? You let the first Popov who pokes his head up with flags have a nice long burst of m.g. fire. Then the whole attack will fall apart. Because that Popov will undoubtedly be the company or battalion commander. And the Popovs go ape-shit when they've got nobody to give 'em orders.'

'Flank 'em – always flank 'em. One Tiger is good enough to take on a whole company of T-34s from the flank. Sus-pension, turret ring, engine cowling – you can pick 'em off one by one from the flank. You'll really have 'em by the juicy nuts. But remember this, the T-34's glacis plate is as tough as that of the Tiger. So if you don't want to die for Folk, Fatherland and Führer earlier than you're going to do anyway, remember that flank, *Flank* . . .'

And so it went on. Von Dodenburg found that Karin

Schmeer's exciting nubile body could hardly keep him awake, just as Sergeant Schulze discovered that her mother's Schnitzel and fried potatoes had begun to lose their attraction, whereas Metzger's suspicions of his Lore were muted somewhat by his fear that the intensive training meant the Battalion was going to be sent to the Eastern Front yet once more.

And Sergeant Metzger was quite correct in his fears. On the 20th June, 1943, battalion commanders and their company commanders were summoned urgently to divisional headquarters at Bielefeld for an immediate briefing by the divisional commander himself.

Sepp Dietrich, the stocky, tough ex-World War I tank sergeant, who had formed the 'Bodyguard' way back in the old days of the Party's fight for power, was in his usual swaggering, quick-witted Bavarian form, helped no doubt by the half a bottle of schnapps he had usually consumed by midday.

'Gentlemen,' he began without any preliminaries, as soon as the officers had settled down in the map room, 'the High Command has really given us a juicy one this time.' He struck the big wall map of the central section of the Russian Front. 'We've got the point with the *Gross-Deutschland*.[2] Our initial target is Prokhorovka so that we can outflank Kursk. When we've done that – and Jesus, Mary, Joseph, we shall do it with 700 vehicles under command including 100 Tigers – we'll push forward to link up with Model's army coming down from the north.' He picked up the glass of Korn which the orderly always kept close to his right hand, and downed it in one gulp. 'Most of you have cured your throat ache, I see. But there'll be some other kind of

2. An elite motorised division, which although it did not belong to the SS, had the privilege of wearing an armband as did the SS divisions (transl.)

tin[3] and promotion in this one for the lot of you.' His brown eyes twinkled merrily and he stuck out his cleft bully boy's jaw aggressively. 'I want a corps out of this one, gentlemen, so I want no-one slipping up. Or by the Great Whore of Buxtehude, I'll want to know why! Understood?'

'Understood, General!' they roared back in unison, including the Vulture who had no great respect for Dietrich's talent as a commander.

'Good. But I don't want you to get the impression that this is going to be a nice little comfortable Viennese waltz. The Soviets have got tremendous defences south of Kursk.' He slapped the map with his bruiser's fist. 'They've dug themselves everywhere in their hedgehogs.[4] According to the Old Fox's[5] men, they're expecting a tank attack in the area so their plan it to let the tanks swing by their strongpoints and wait for the follow-up infantry. Good, let the bastards wait.' He smiled, showing his strong white teeth under the trim little moustache. 'They can wait till the Day of Judgement as far as I am concerned. The Bodyguard will take its infantry with it on the backs of the Tigers. When we've linked up with Model's Army and the Popovs are still scratching their hairy backsides and wondering what happened to the Germanskis, then we can start sorting out their fine hedgehogs. All the same you'd better hear what exactly the Popovs have got waiting for us south of Kursk.' He raised his voice and barked, 'Kraemer, come and play my Chief-of-Staff. And Orderly, bring me another goddam drink before I die of thirst!'

With a sigh Kraemer, Dietrich's elegant Regular Army Chief-of-Staff, who had often confided to the Vulture that

3. SS slang for decorations (transl.)
4. Fortified positions, manned by a company of infantry with four or five pieces of artillery, linked together in a rough line (transl.)
5. Name given to Admiral Canaris, the sly head of the German Intelligence Section.

his boss could not even read a map, stepped into the centre of the group and began rattling off the statistics.

'The depth of defence of the Central and Varonezh Fronts on the axes of German attack reach from 120 to 170 kilometres.' Even the hard-bitten battalion commanders of the 'Führer's Fire Brigade' could not fight back their gasps of surprise; but Kraemer did not seem to hear. 'The Soviets have dug some 5000 kilometres of trenches and have laid approximately 400,000 bombs and ground mines. There are some 2,400 anti-tank and 2,700 anti-personnel mines per kilometre of front – six times that of the defence of Moscow and four times that of Stalingrad last year. The Soviets have also given their anti-aircraft defences great attention. According to the Old Fox's spies, they have nine anti-aircraft artillery divisions, plus 40 regiments—'

'Enough, enough,' Dietrich broke in suddenly. 'Christ, Kraemer, do you want to frighten the life out of them?'

'I'm simply giving them the facts, General,' Kraemer said without rancour, as if he had gone through similar scenes many times before.

'Facts!' Dietrich snorted. 'Soldiers can't concern themselves with facts. If they did, they'd never even go into action. They'd be too petrified by the knowledge that, according to the statistics, one of the pieces of shit flying around must have their number on it.' He looked at the assembled officers a rogueish look in his brown eyes. 'Gentlemen, I suggest that since you know what is expected of us in this new mission and – thanks to my little ray of sunshine here, Kraemer – what kind of shitty opposition we can anticipate, you leave here and do what every soldier should before he goes into battle – get a snootful of booze and get himself laid, if he can.' He raised his voice and bellowed, 'Orderly – the drinks!'

A group of white-coated mess waiters came hurrying in,

bearing silver trays of ice-cold glasses of Korn. Hastily they passed them out to the officers.

Sepp Dietrich raised his glass. 'Gentlemen, to the success of Operation Citadel!' he roared.

'*Operation Citadel!*' they bellowed in unison.

In one gulp they downed the fiery spirit. The next instant the room was full of the noise of splintering glass, as officer after officer flung his glass into the stone fireplace.

SEVEN

Von Dodenburg shook his head and the room came into focus. But his vision was still blurred. He shook his head again, a little more forcefully, and wished a second later that he hadn't.

Slowly, carefully, he let his eyes wander round the room. Her clothes were everywhere. The white cotton slip, such as schoolgirls wore, on the floor; her pants screwed into a ball flung on the dresser, as if she hadn't been able to get them off quickly enough; her sweater spreadeagled over the end of the big bed, the arms thrust out, like a headless swimmer.

Karin was still sleeping peacefully, face down on the rumpled stained bed, the feather quilt thrown back impatiently the way children do in their sleep. But there was nothing childlike in the brown-tanned naked body at his side. The dark down revealed from under one raised arm, the plump curve of the breast, the rise of the buttocks and the pubic puff between her spread legs – they all indicated a woman: an experienced woman.

For in spite of her sixteen years, there was nothing sexually immature about Karin Schmeer. When Schulze had deposited him, weaving drunkenly from Bielefeld, outside

69

her door, she had not hesitated; ignoring the big-breasted maid's shocked looks, she had almost dragged him up to her bedroom and started pulling off her clothes with excited trembling hands.

Thereafter the night had been one frantic, frenzied bout of lovemaking after another, as if the teenaged girl could not get enough to satiate the burning lust which tore at her body. Finally he had pleaded he must sleep and although she had cried bitterly, he had drifted into a dream-racked sleep in which he saw the battalion standing completely naked on some God-forsaken burning Russian steppe while monstrous Soviet tanks mowed them down calmly and deliberately as if engaged in a peacetime exercise.

At his side Karin groaned. She turned, opened her eyes and put her brown arms round his neck. 'Kiss me,' she whispered through cracked, scummed lips.

He did so. But there was no conviction in his kiss, and she knew it. She drew back and surveyed him for a moment. Then she pushed back a lock of the long blonde hair which had fallen over her brow.

'What's the matter?' she asked soberly, without any emotion.

He shrugged his naked shoulders. 'This I suppose.'

'Why?'

'Somehow it's wrong. I mean you're only a schoolgirl and I'm an SS officer. I've had experience—' He broke off a little helplessly, not able to find the right words to express himself.

'Don't you think I've had other men, Kuno?' she asked.

'Obviously. But what if your father found out? What would he think of my – well you know?'

She grinned cynically and ran her hands over her full breasts contemptuously. 'Him! He doesn't care. All he cares about it filling his own pockets and those Jewish whores

70

down in the old city, who let him play out his dirty little tricks because they're scared to death he might put them in the camps if they didn't.'

'Filling his pockets – Jewish whores – in National Socialist Germany!' von Dodenburg stuttered.

She smiled at his bewilderment, and not taking her eyes off him, reached out for a cigarette. 'A German woman does not use make-up or smoke,'[1] she said and lit it. Blowing out a long stream of contented blue smoke, she added. 'Don't look at me like that, Captain von Dodenburg! *Shit!* Where have you been all these last years since 1939, eh?'

'At the front.'

'The front – oh, there!' she said carelessly, as if it were as far away as Mars. 'I understand. But you must understand too, that this is Germany 1943. Things have changed.'

'How have things changed?' he persisted, although he could already feel her free hand fondling him, a look of dreamy amusement on her young face.

'Just changed. People are out for themselves.' Her cunning hands were stroking him into excitement now with soft feathery movements like those of some Parisian whore.

'You are just a child, what do you know?' he persisted, trying to fight back the desire which had begun to bubble up within his loins once more.

'Child,' she whispered huskily. 'Put your arms around me and I'll show you whether I am a child or not.'

He attempted to push her hand away, but she held on to him tightly, as if she could not bear to let go of this source of intense delight. He could feel her body begin to tremble with desire.

'Come on,' she urged and slowly began to open her long brown legs.

1. A catch-phrase used in wartime Germany to mock Nazi thinking on the role of women in the Third Reich (transl.)

In spite of himself, he threw his right leg over her, ready to mount. But fate had decreed otherwise. He would never make love to Karin Schmeer again. Just as she began to draw up her legs to receive him, there was a thunderous knock on the door and a well-known voice called.

'It's only me, sir.'

Next moment Schulze burst in, clad only in his boots and vest, a half empty bottle of Korn in one hand, the other clasping the enormous right breast of the hopelessly drunk and giggling maid, who was completely naked.

'Sir—' he stopped suddenly when he realized what von Dodenburg was about to do. 'The Prussian don't shoot that quickly, sir!' he cried, a huge grin spreading over his cheeky waterfront face.

'What the devil do you think you're up to, Schulze?' von Dodenburg yelled angrily, hastily pulling the feather quilt over himself and the girl, her legs still raised expectantly.

'Don't get angry, sir. I'm just doing my duty – sorry that I had to interrupt you in yours,' he added with a knowing grin at the girl.

'Get on with it. What damn duty?'

'Dehn, you know him, sir?'

Von Dodenburg nodded.

'Well, sir, I told him last night where to find us if anything came up.'

'And?'

'It's come up, sir – like a couple of other things this night, no doubt.'

'What, man. Spit it out!'

'We're off. Dehn just got me and the maid here out of the pit to tell us. Now he's waiting outside with the Volkswagen.'

'Heaven, arse and twine, man,' von Dodenburg exploded. 'What are you talking about? Where are we off to?'

'To the front, sir! *We march in twelve hours' time.*'

72

The growing knowledge that the Battalion would be going to the front again soon finally galvanised Metzger into action. On that same morning, he slipped out of the Battalion Office and instead of going for his 'second breakfast' of a beer and a gin, he hurried to County Leader Schmeer's headquarters.

Schmeer's secretary, a hard-faced bitch who had plenty of wood stacked in front of her door, as he couldn't help noticing, shook her head when he asked to see her boss.

'The County Leader is a very busy man. One can't just see him like that.'

'I can,' Metzger snapped, made bold by his knowledge and his sense of urgency. 'Tell him it's damned important.'

She sniffed, but did as he asked, swishing out with an arse on her like a ten dollar horse. She seemed to be away a long time, leaving him with a baggy-eyed bust of the Iron Chancellor; a poster of the Führer sitting on a white horse, dressed in medieval armour and carrying a swastika banner; and a picture of a little boy urinating into a pool with beneath the old caption: 'Don't drink water – it's bad for you!'

Finally the secretary with the big arse returned.

'The County Leader will give you five minutes now,' she said.

'And I'll give him fifty years, if he's not shitty well careful,' Metzger grunted as he elbowed his way past her.

Inside the inner office, he snapped to attention and bellowed, 'Heil Hitler, County Leader!'

'Heil Hitler,' Schmeer said wearily, barely raising his hand. 'Not so loud, Metzger, if you please. I was on the piss last night. Too much beer – and the other.'

Metzger's grim look did not relax. 'I'm not surprised, County Leader. You like your little parties, don't you. Up the cups – cheers New Year, the night's going to be cold!'

Schmeer looked up at Metzger's big, angry face in bewilderment.

'What the hell's the matter with you, Metzger. Haven't you got all your cups in your cupboard or something?'

'Oh, yes, Mr County Leader. I'm all right in the head. It's your head you should worry about – you and your girlfriends named Sarah.'

'Sarah who?'

'Don't try to take me on your arm,' Metzger snapped angrily. 'I saw you with that Yiddish whore the other night.'

'Oh that,' Schmeer said easily.

'Yes, *that*! What do you think the Gestapo would say if they knew that a senior member of the Party was having sexual intercourse with a Jewess!'

'If you only knew what the Gestapo did in this town, Metzger,' Schmeer sneered, completely unmoved.

Metzger ignored the comment. 'While men like me are at the front,' he threw a contemptuous glance at Schmeer's War Service Cross Second Class, 'you base stallions interfere with our women and not only that you commit racial impurity with Jewesses.'

A light dawned in Schmeer's reddened eyes. 'So that's it, Metzger. You think me and your Lore,' he didn't complete the sentence, but his thumb thrust obscenely between his two middle fingers made his meaning quite clear.

'Yes, I sodding well do and I intend to stop it.'

Schmeer tugged the end of his long nose. 'Not that I wouldn't have minded, Metzger. Your Lore's got a fine pair of lungs on her. All that meat and no potatoes,' he chuckled. 'That's what we say in East Westphalia.' He sighed. 'But I'm afraid a better man than me was there first, Metzger.'

'*What?*' Metzger exploded. 'What do you mean?'

'What I say. Someone else was getting a piece of it before I got to know your Lore.'

'Who?' roared Metzger.

'That little fellow in your house. Haven't you ever noticed the way his shoulders are bent. That's always a sign a man's got plenty of meat in his breeches.'

'*Who?*'

'Who?' echoed Schmeer, his fat face one huge malicious grin. 'Can't you see what's going on right under your big nose?'

'*Who?*' Metzger yelled, his face crimson, the veins standing out at his temples.

'That little spaghetti-eater, of course.'

'*Mario?*'

'That's right, that's him.'

The bedsprings were going like overheated pistons as he flung open the door and started pelting up the stairs two at a time; and he didn't need to be told that Lore was not changing the bed sheets.

'Great crap on the Christmas Tree,' he roared to no one in particular. 'Thank God, I've not got my duty pistol with me. 'I'll shoot both the fornicating bastards!'

He flung open the door of his flat. He could see right through the place into the bedroom and what he saw was worse than he could ever have imagined.

Lore was on her back, her plump legs stuck in the air, the sweat pouring off her naked flesh, her mouth like that of a dying fish gasping for air, while the undersized muscular, dark-skinned spaghetti eater jumped up and down on top of her soft white body, as if he were trying to pump her full of gas with the thing that he had stuck into her dark cavity. And the way Lore's eye were rolling crazily under her disarranged hair there was plenty of it too.

'You bitch!' he exploded. 'You shitty fornicating bitch!'

Mario started. He swung a look behind him and his dark

face went a shade of green. 'Lore,' he cried in alarm and raised his upper body from her. 'It's him – your man!'

'Shut up,' she gasped in ecstasy and pulled him down on her again. 'It's lovely, my little cheetah. More!'

'*More* – I'll give you fucking well *more*!' Metzger yelled, beside himself with rage, as she clung to Mario, her legs wrapped round his back while he writhed desperately to free himself.

With a heave he pulled himself off her plump white body. Slowly she opened her eyes and stared up stupidly at her husband's crimson enraged face.

'You,' she breathed.

'Who did you shitting well expect – bloody Father Christmas!'

He doubled up his big fist and prepared to smash it in her face. But he never completed the action. From down below came the honking of a car horn and an urgent impatient official voice shouted up the stairs.

'Sergeant Metzger – alert, alert! Report to the barracks at once! We march – we march.'

TWO: OPERATION CITADEL

'It's been an excellent day. Obviously we caught the Popovs with their knickers down.'

Major Geier to Capt. von Dodenburg,
July 5th, 1943.

ONE

'What a sodding awful time of day to go and get yourself killed,' Schulze grumbled, staring at the silent endless steppe in front of them. 'Midday in the month of July. At least it's cool in a dawn attack.'

Von Dodenburg crouched next to him in the parched yellow Russian grass, pushed back his helmet, wiped the sweat off his brow and said, 'My dear thick Schulze. The Popovs are accustomed to us attacking at dawn. This time we're doing it at late afternoon, because we want to catch them with their Soviet knickers down.'

'I've got to see that first, sir,' Schulze persisted.

'You will – never fear.'

Von Dodenburg cast a glance behind into the hollow to check if his company was still alert in spite of the heavy oppressive summer. They were, despite the Russian sun beating remorselessly down on the Tigers, quivering in blue burning waves over the metal. But the faint wind had dropped now and the flies and sand fleas were at work again. The men of Wotan scratched their bodies with sullen angry persistence.

Von Dodenburg prevented himself from beginning to scratch his own infested body by an effort of will and glanced yet once again at his big issue watch. But the Vulture beat him to it.

'Thirteen fifty,' he rasped and rose to his feet, riding crop – his only weapon – held firmly in his little hand. Von Dodenburg joined him. If the Popovs spotted them, they would assume that the two Germans were on some sort of reconnaissance mission, he told himself. They would not suspect that the best part of two elite divisions were massed by the long line of ridges.

But there was no sign of the Russians in their line of fortified hedgehogs [1] some eight hundred metres away.

'Sleeping off their midday meal,' von Dodenburg observed, 'Like any self-respecting member of the great working masses should.'

'Recovering more likely from that cheap vodka they're always drinking, von Dodenburg.'

'All the same, it looks good sir,' von Dodenburg said, covering the immense plain with his binoculars and not seeing a sign of movement save for a thin column of blue smoke in the far distance.

'I think we've caught them this time on the hop.'

'Yes, I agree. I have a feeling that we're going to pull it off without too much trouble. Even that sergeant who runs the division' – he was referring to Dietrich as von Dodenburg knew – 'can't make a balls up of this one.'

'Let us pray you're right, sir,' von Dodenburg said with sudden fervour. 'The whole future of the Reich depends on success at Kursk.'

The Vulture sniffed and tugged at the end of his monstrous nose which had been burned a salmon pink by the hot Russian sun.

'Yes, and my chances of getting a regiment too, it must be remembered, my dear von Dodenburg.'

The younger officer opened his mouth to protest at such cynicism when it was obvious that Operation Citadel would be the decisive campaign of the whole long bloody Russian war, but the Vulture did not give him the opportunity to do so. He tugged his officer's whistle from his jacket and blew a shrill blast on it.

1. Fortified positions, manned by a company of infantry with four or five pieces of artillery, linked together in a rough line (transl.)

The men waiting below reacted immediately, as if they were only too eager to get started. While von Dodenburg doubled back to his company, Schulze at his heels, the panzer grenadiers started to slide into their combat packs, slinging their machine pistols over their chests. NCOs began to hand out extra stick grenades, which were seized eagerly as if they were ice cream cones. Behind them the tankers clambered up the sides of the steel monsters and swung themselves easily into the hatches. Here and there the more nervous urinated for the umpteenth time against the Tigers, while the drivers made their usual comment: 'What do you think this is – a sodding St Pauli piss-corner or something?'

Schulze stuck a last piece of the special combat-issue chocolate into his big mouth and chewing mightily, he strolled towards von Dodenburg's command tank, as if they were about to set off on some routine mission and not on an attack against the greatest mass fortification system in history.

'First Company, ready – sir!' von Dodenburg yelled above the noise, raising his hand high into the air.

Vulture touched his riding crop to his helmet in acknowledgement.

'Second Company ready – sir!' Schwarz yelled.

And so it went on. The Vulture took one last look at their tough confident young faces, as if he were seeing them for the very first time.

'Start up!' he yelled.

The drivers pressed their starter buttons as one. Everywhere there were thick, asthmatic coughs. Thin smoke began to stream out of the Tigers' exhausts. With a roar the first engine burst into life. And the next. Suddenly the still summer afternoon was hideous with the noise. Hastily the panzer grenadiers clambered onto the tanks like a crowd of schoolkids boarding an excursion bus scared of being left behind.

On the stroke of two there was an earth shaking roar behind them which drowned the noise of the tanks into insignificance. With a hoarse exultant scream, the whole weight of the SS Panzer Corps artillery sped over their heads to tear into the Soviet first line, bursting with a mighty antiphonal crash. As they rumbled to the start-line just below the brow of the rise, the thunder of the guns continued. Flight after flight of shells streamed over their heads in a vicious anger. Their first red-hot sighing became a scream – a monstrous baleful scream. The scream rose in fury, elemental yet controlled. Before them the first Soviet line disappeared in smoke, the clouds rising straight into the still air.

The heavy artillery moved on to the second line. Now the six-barrelled rocket-mortars took over. From their positions two hundred metres behind the Wotan Battalion, the gunners pressed the buttons that activated the electric firing mechanism. There was the sound of someone hitting the bass notes on a piano. It was followed by a grating noise – like a diamond being run across glass. Suddenly the air above them was full of clusters of heavy canopies. With tremendous crashes they landed among the hedgehogs. This was it. The mortar men would keep any surviving Soviet in his hole until the tanks with their loads of crouching panzer grenadiers were among the hedgehogs, ready to mop up.

'Roll 'em!' the Vulture's voice rasped metallicly over the radio.

Automatically von Dodenburg pressed both his radio and intercom buttons.

'Forward – first company,' he commanded. 'Gunners prepare to fire smoke once the barrage lifts!'

As he pulled the turret flap and pulled the periscope

towards him, he could hear the other company commanders rapping out the same orders.

Schulze, who had taken over from the driver, for the first attack, let out his clutch. The Tiger lumbered forward. The next instant it had breasted the rise, showering the tanks behind it with rubble and dust.

Von Dodenburg sucked in his breath and felt as if something had suddenly scorched his tonsils. The Popov first line was on fire. Angry blue flames licked up everywhere among the wall of dust. But still the deadly rockets kept striking the hedgehogs. Surely, he told himself, no one could live in that hell!

But they could. A zinc-like light bared itself to his right front. A wild tearing struck the air. Like the sound of a huge piece of canvas being ripped apart, the first Soviet shell zipped by his Tiger. Suddenly his right ear seemed to go deaf. Angrily he banged his right earphone with the flat of his hand.

'Get ready for smoke, gunner,' he ordered the gunner hunched into his scope, his own voice sounding strangely distorted. 'The Ivans are reacting.'

'Sir!' the gunner snapped, his free hand cranking the turret with its long hooded gun from left to right, ready to fire in an instant, if a hostile appeared.

Suddenly von Dodenburg spotted the first T-34, emerging from the smoke.

'*Popovs!*' he yelled over the radio, warning the rest of the company. 'Gunner – cannon traverse right – two o'clock . . . on!'

Hastily the gunner swung the 88 round.

'On!' Von Dodenburg took a quick look through the periscope. The T-34 was neatly outlined against the crosswires of the sight. '*Fire!*' he yelled.

The gunner squeezed the firing bar. Automatically von

Dodenburg opened his mouth against the blast. The great tank shuddered and reared back on its rear sprockets. Acrid yellow smoke filled the turret. The blast whipped against von Dodenburg's face and next instant the breech opened and the smoking yellow cartridge case came clattering onto the deck. With his left hand he loaded a fresh round and with his right pressed the smoke-extractor.

'Fire again – brew the bastard up!' he yelled, as the smoke cleared to reveal the T-34 had stopped.

Slowly, terribly slowly, the Popov gunner was trying to swing his 76 mm round, as if he were already slumped dying over the breech. Von Dodenburg's gunner did not give him a chance. The 88 spoke again. The T-34 reared up like a live thing. Its right track flapped out behind it. Suddenly the turret lurched forward and its gun sunk, as if it were an animal whose head had been severed.

'Stop firing!' von Dodenburg yelled, eager not to waste any more precious ammunition on the T-34.

But Schwarz's voice screamed over the radio to his own gunner. '*Hit him – hit him again* – I want to see the Soviet bastard burn!'

To von Dodenburg's right there was the dry flat bark of an 88. The shell struck the crippled T-34 squarely in its fuel tank. It jetted orange flame, surrounded by thick black oily smoke. Still no crew appeared.

But Schwarz was not to be cheated of his prey. 'Keep on that machine gun,' von Dodenburg heard him command against the crackling background of the static.

A small dark figure appeared in the cupola. For a moment he hesitated, the blue flames licking up about him everywhere. Then he made up his mind. He toppled into the dusty grass and rolling frantically, tried to extinguish the flames. Schwarz did not give him a chance.

'Gunner,' he ordered eagerly. 'Spandau! Ivan near tank – fire!'

Schwarz's gunner must have hesitated, for von Dodenburg heard the officer cry crazily: 'I said fire, you shitty green-beak you!' The next instant a flat angry burst of tracer zipped across the burning steppe.

The gunner could not miss at that range. The Ivan's spine curved frighteningly, his black-charred hands clawed the air, and he fell back screaming. The gunner's next burst caught the driver fighting his way out of the escape hatch. It took his head off. On the turret, a third crew member flung up his hands in fearful surrender. The plea did not help him. At one hundred metres range, the gunner poured a burst into his defenceless body. It disappeared in a bloody broken welter, as if someone had just thrust it into a mincing machine.

At the driving controls the big Hamburger Schulze gulped and said thickly, 'Well, I'll crap in my hat! We're really getting off to a good start, ain't we, sir?'

Von Dodenburg did not reply, but as they rattled by the burning T-34 and its slaughtered young crew, he looked away.

As soon as the rocket barrage ended, the Russians reacted quickly. Salvo after salvo – ragged though they were, as if the Russian gunners had been caught off guard – rained down on the advancing battalion. Almost immediately, the terrifying 'Stalin Organs' [2] joined in. But their aim was wild and they concentrated on plastering the empty positions which the Wotan had just left.

'Smoke!' von Dodenburg yelled urgently. 'For Chrissake – smoke everybody!'

The gunners needed no urging. The first Soviet line was

2. Soviet rocket-mortars.

still two hundred metres away and they were completely exposed now. Quickly they fired their smoke dischargers. The black containers soared clumsily into the air. They exploded almost immediately, throwing a thick white stream of smoke ahead of the ragged line of tanks. In a matter of seconds the Wotan was wreathed in a dense mist.

Frustrated of their prey, the Soviet gunners intensified their fire, knowing they must stop the Tigers before they got into the first line. The air filled with the hysterical screams of the Stalin Organs. From the rear the heavies crumped throatily, over and over again. And as the distance between the attackers and defenders narrowed, the Russians began to take a toll of the Tigers. Suddenly the radio began reporting their casualties on all sides.

'Two m.g.s bothering me from left flank – all my Panzer Grenadiers hit. Like a skating rink with blood up on the deck . . .' . . . 'Track gone, I'm sitting out here like a spare penis at a wedding. Need protection urgently . . .' 'Engine damaged. Can't see a hand in front of you for fumes. Can I bail out? . . .'

Then suddenly they had burst through their own smoke screen and with the Soviet barrage still hitting the ground behind them harmlessly, they were only one hundred metres from the enemy line.

The ground was pitted everywhere with huge brown holes. The few trees there were, were stripped white of their bark, their boughs hanging down like shattered limbs. But there were still Soviet troops alive and willing to fight among the shattered wreckage of the front line. Almost immediately the signal flares hushed into the burning air everywhere. The Soviet machine guns opened up angrily. Lead pattered against the Tigers' metal sides like heavy summer rain. But there was no stopping them now.

The 1st Company's flame-thrower tank darted out its

deadly tongue. Flame licked its way around the first bunker. The paint on its wall bubbled suddenly like heated toffee. Its machine gun stopped firing. Two T-34s came rumbling frantically towards them. In their haste and fear they crashed into each other. The next instant a luck shot from the flank whacked into them and went through both. Nobody bailed out.

'Spread out – First Company, for God's sake spread out!' von Dodenburg yelled desperately over the radio.

Not a moment too soon. A Soviet 57 mm, concealed behind what looked like a barn, opened up at seventy-five metres range. Von Dodenburg could actually see the glowing white AP[3] shell heading towards them, gaining speed every second.

'Gunner – target two—'

The crump of the tank's 88 crashed into his words. The gunner had seen the anti-tank gun before he had. The 57 mm disappeared in a ball of ugly red and yellow flame, its crew dark pieces of flotsam flying through the air. Below them, Schulze wrenched at the steering rods. The Tiger swung round violently, sending a surprised von Dodenburg careening against the hull. His mouth filled with salt-tasting blood. But he had no time for his cut face. The Soviet shell had missed them. But another T-34 was roaring in out of the smoke, only a matter of fifty metres away.

'Gunner,' he cried in an agony of urgent fear. 'Three o'clock – Popov tank!'

Schulze, reading von Dodenburg's mind, crashed home the reverse gear. The Tiger thundered out of the way, cutting into a group of Soviet infantrymen carrying a rocket-launcher. They disappeared under the tank's great metal tracks screaming, to be flung out at the other side like pieces of chopped beef. The Tiger crew did not even notice. The

3. Armour-piercing shell (transl.)

T-34's shell whistled past their turret. The 60-ton monster rocked as if it had been made of paper and not steel. The next instant the T-34 shot over the top of the burning bunker, revealing the whole length of its underarmoured belly.

'Gunner – for Chrissake, get him in the knackers!' Schulze yelled from below.

'Now – now,' von Dodenburg urged, ready to feed in the next shell. The gunner pressed the pedal. The turret swung round. In the sight, the twin triangles met. The belly of the T-34 blocked out everything else. It seemed to fill the whole world. Peering through his own periscope, von Dodenburg could see every rusty rivet, every mud and oil-stained bolt.

The gunner pulled the firing lever. There was the grate of metal striking metal. Even through the thickness of their own turret armour, their ears rang with the enormous din. The T-34 rose into the air and fell the next instant on its back.

Their Tigers pushed on. With Dodenburg in the lead, the 1st Company rolled over dead and dying Russians, crushing them deep into the very earth, which suddenly began to turn to dusty red with their blood. From the cunning camouflaged 'readiness bunkers' behind the pillboxes, Ivans in dark-coloured underwear came streaming out, screaming at the tops of their voices. They didn't have a chance. Von Dodenburg's twin spandaus burst into them at 800 rounds per minute. They fell like crazy nine-pins. Within seconds they were piled up six deep at the doors of the bunkers. As the first wave rolled by, some one tossed a couple of incendiary grenades into the nearest heap. The Ivans began to burn fiercely, with those still alive struggling vainly to get out of the funeral pyre.

A small T-60 Soviet tank came careering round a corner. Four 88 mm shells hit it simultaneously. It disappeared, as if it had never even existed. Everywhere now the Ivans were throwing down their weapons and beginning to surrender. But the men of Wotan had no time for prisoners.

'Come on over here, you bastards,' von Dodenburg heard a voice cry over the radio – he couldn't identify whose. 'We'll flatten you like floor mats!'

Whoever it was, he made good his promise. A stream of machine gun poured into the Russians. They scattered panic-stricken. Too late. They went down in their dozens.

They roared on. But von Dodenburg trying to bring some order into his hopelessly snarled up company knew they weren't through the first line completely yet. Cursing viciously over the radio and repeatedly shouting at members of other companies who were getting into his frequency, he managed to extend his two flanks and prevent the centre group of Tigers from bunching too much. He succeeded just in time. Just as they had cleared the last of the bunkers, leaving behind them a bloody wake of crushed dead and dying Ivans, the smoke dissipated to reveal a fantastic spectacle.

An arrowhead of some twenty T-34s advancing towards them, their headlights blazing, their tracks muffled by the thick dust so that they looked like noiseless spectres. Von Dodenburg pressed his throat mike swiftly.

'Schulze, give me everything you've got!'

Schulze responded at once. He shot the gear lever through the thirty-odd forward gears the Tiger had. The 60-ton monster gathered speed.

'Traverse right,' the young SS officer yelled urgently. 'We've got to flank the right wing!'

The sweat-soaked gunner, his uniform back a greasy black with perspiration, swung the long gun through an arc, while von Dodenburg tore another shell from the rack in front of him. He pressed the smoke extractor button again. The distance between the two lines of tanks was narrowing now. Behind him he knew that his own Tigers would be forming an arrow formation too, forced by his own manoeuvre to the right of the T-34s. Next to him, the gunner, his eye pressed to the rubber sight, began to call out the distance.

'Three hundred metres . . . two hundred metres . . . one hundred and fifty.'

But it was the Soviets who fired first. Suddenly there was a blinding light from the closest T-34. A second later the sound of the explosion erupted into the silence. Blast engulfed them, followed by a breathless suction.

The gunner yelled out as if he had been hit while the Tiger rocked like a ship in a gale at sea as the 76 mm shell swept by them harmlessly. But it was just fear, not pain. In the next instant he pulled the firing lever and their own shell shot out towards the Soviets.

What happened next was a confused mess of muzzle flashes, the scrunch of metal against metal, the shriek of ricochets, and the great whoosh of fuel tanks exploding and another tank dying in a great black funeral pyre of oily smoke. Twice they heard the rapping of death on their turret like the beak of some monstrous raven, as shells careened off it, leaving a faint glowing redness in the yellow darkness as the shell worked its way along the metal before glancing off harmlessly. But in each case their Soviet opponents paid for their temerity, their T-34s being brewed up immediately, spewing their metallic lava towards the burning sky.

How long the tank battle lasted, von Dodenburg never knew. It might have been hours, but it also might only have been minutes. More than once he had been forced to open the turret, risking the danger of some Soviet suicide squad armed with Molotov cocktails, in order to clear the cupola of the yellow acrid fumes; and each time as he risked a glance about him all he could see was dying tanks – German and Russian – everywhere.

And then suddenly the fight went out of what was left of the Russians. Von Dodenburg caught a glimpse of the Soviet regimental commander as he tried to rally his wavering force with his little signal flags. But a lucky Spandau burst ripped out his chest and as he slumped dead over the red star decorating his turret, his men panicked.

The T-34 drivers spun their vehicles round in their tracks. A couple barely missed crashing into each other in their panic-stricken haste. Everywhere the Germans cheered – von Dodenburg could hear them over the crackling radio. Swiftly they started to plaster the retreating T-34s. Now they were easy meat, their under-armoured engines clearly exposed. But their radio link must have been still functioning. For just as the men of Wotan had begun ranging in, the Stalin organs to the rear opened up again and plastered the battlefield with smoke and high explosion.

'Hastily von Dodenburg pressed his throat mike. 'All right,' he yelled, retire – *retire!*'

'A German soldier never gives up ground,' an unknown young voice cried angrily over the radio.

'You'll be telling me next you believe in the stork and Father Christmas, you silly young shit?' It was Schulze, shouting into the intercom in his thick waterfront accent. 'Get yer arse out of here before the Popovs cut off yer sodding, dumb eggs – with a blunt penknife!'

Suiting his own actions to his words, he spun the sixty ton monster round and sent it clattering back the way it had come. Behind him the survivors of the 1st Company did the same. The first day of the great new offensive was over.

Schwarz's Second Company was shooting the few Ivan

prisoners when the 1st Company rattled to a stop among the Soviet hedgehogs. It was all very scientific and routine. Occasionally one of the shaven-headed teenage Siberians whimpered and refused to move forward towards the liquidation squad, made up of Schwarz, his bare arms bloodied to the elbows, and a couple of his senior NCOs. A rifle butt between the shoulders or crashed against the back of his shaven skull soon persuaded the man to move forward. But mostly they accepted their fate impassively, no emotion showing on their flat yellow faces, as the liquidators placed their Walthers behind the Siberians' right ears and blew them into a Soviet paradise.

All the same von Dodenburg did not like the look of the pile of corpses stacked awkwardly by Schwarz's command Tiger, their limbs thrust out extravagantly. He looked the other way as he marched up to a waiting Vulture, clicked his heels together and reported in the parade ground style the CO expected from his officers even in the middle of a battlefield.

'Three vehicles completely knocked out, two suitable for recovery. Casualties – ten officers and men killed, fifteen wounded!'

The Vulture touched his overlarge cap with his riding crop. 'Good, von Dodenburg. Not bad at all.' He took the yonger man and steered him away from where Schwarz was about to place his bloodied pistol against an impassive-faced Siberian's skull yet once again. 'Let's get away from here. We've had enough noise for this day – and besides those damned Chinks are lousy anyway. I'd hate to get their lice on me.'

'Yessir.'

Obediently von Dodenburg walked along beside his CO automatically stepping over the Soviet dead sprawled out in

92

the ruins or skirting a new shell crater, while the Vulture put him in the picture.

'It's been an excellent day. Obviously we caught the Popovs with their knickers down. Apparently they thought the main attack would come from the North – from Colonel-General Model. According to that Sergeant who controls our destiny – Kraemer was on the radio-phone to me a quarter of an hour ago. We've penetrated the 52nd Guards Rifle Brigade or Division, we don't know which yet. You know how slow Gehlen's Intelligence is.'[4]

Von Dodenburg didn't, but he nodded his agreement, as if he did. He stepped over a Popov whose face had been burned completely away, leaving a black congealed mass, streaked with dried blood and two scarlet pools where his eyes had once been.

'My guess is that we've split the Sixth Guards Army and that Prokhorovka will fall like a ripe apple tomorrow.'

Despite his utter weariness, von Dodenburg's face beamed beneath its oily mask. 'That's really good news,' he said enthusiastically. 'But what about Kempf's detachments?'

The Vulture stared at the burning plain, littered with crippled tanks now silhouetted stark black against the blood-red ball of the setting sun.

'They're not providing the flank coverage Dietrich antici-pated they would. After all they do not belong to the elite of the Armed SS, do they?'

Von Dodenburg dismissed the Vulture's underlying cyni-cism. 'Oh, let the damn flanks take care of themselves, sir. We've always done it before, why should we worry now.' He forced a tired laugh. 'The Wotan will move so fast that the Popovs won't be able to find our flanks.'

The Vulture grinned faintly at the younger man's un-

4. General Gehlen, head of the Foreign Armies East, the Wehr-macht's Intelligence service dealing with the East.

inhibited enthusiasm. He raised his shoulders wearily. 'I'm sure you're right, von Dodenburg. Very well, see your men are bedded down soon. We shall move out at dawn, push through the village of Pokrovka and go hell-for-leather for Prokhorovka—'

He broke off suddenly. To their front a small group of men from the tank recovery section were using a foot pump to clean out the inside of a shot-up Tiger. Up to now a stream of pink liquid had been spurting out of the drainage holes – blood mixed with water. But for some reason there was a blockage and pump as they would, no further liquid came out. Casually Vulture, followed by an utterly weary von Dodenburg, went over to the recovery crew.

'What's the matter, corporal?' the CO asked the sweating corporal at the pump.

'The sod won't flush, sir,' he gasped and stopped his efforts. In spite of the blessed coolness of the evening, the sweat was still pouring from his naked chest.

'You've got a blockage then, haven't you. Why don't you go inside and find it?'

'Well, sir.' Suddenly the skinny bare-chested corporal was embarrassed.

'She took a direct hit with a 76 mm.' He indicated the gleaming metallic hole neatly skewered through the Tiger's turret. 'The crew was all dead when we got the pieces out and we sort of—'

'You're scared, aren't you?' the Vulture broke into his lame explanation. 'That's it, isn't it?'

Impatiently the Vulture pushed him to one side and swung himself on the blackened turret. 'I want this vehicle back in action by dawn,' he said looking down at the crew. 'I've got no time for your petty fears.'

And with that he clambered inside the cupola. For a few minutes they could hear him rummaging around in the dark charred chaos inside. Suddenly the blood-and-water mixture started to run again from the drainage holes.

The Vulture reappeared at the turret, his enormous nose wrinkled up, obviously disgusted by the stench of the tank's interior. He held up one hand. Hanging from it by the hair was a head. With a sudden hot spasm of nausea, von Dodenburg recognised it. It was that of Corporal Dehn of his own Company.

'This was the thing blocking the main hole,' the Vulture said in completely normal tone. Almost casually he tossed the head aside. The recovery crew ducked hastily as the gruesome thing sailed by them. The Vulture stepped down, dusting his bloodied hands on his breeches. 'Now get on with it. We've got exactly seven more hours till dawn.'

The recovery crew began pumping again as if their very lives depended on it, while behind them in the dust the sightless eyes of Corporal Dehn's skull stared into a darkening sky.

Thirty odd kilometres from where the recovery crew hosed out the damaged Tiger that night, the squat, bald representative of the Soviet Military Council faced Lieutenant General Katukov and his staff in their underground bunker. The Commander of the Soviet First Tank Army had just ordered that two regiments of his assault guns drawn from his reserves of 1,300 armoured vehicles, should go to the aid of the badly hit Sixth Guards Army. Now he wondered what the little civilian politico, disguised as a major general in the Red Army, would want from him next.

But surprisingly enough the politico wanted nothing else. He let his cunning peasant eyes run round the grave pale faces of the assembled staff officers.

'The next two or three days will be terrible, comrades,' he said slowly, warningly. 'Either we hold or the Germans will take Kursk. They are putting everything on one card.' He raised his pudgy forefinger in a gesture that the whole world would come to know and fear one day. 'It's a matter of life or death for them. We must take care to see that they break their necks.' Major General Nikita Khrushchev, one day to be dictator of all Russia, chuckled throatily, the jowls of his broad peasant face wobbling as he did so.

Suddenly he raised his right knee and snapped his powerful hands across it. 'Just like that, comrades,' he growled, not taking his eyes from their faces. 'That is how we will deal with the Fritzes. Understand?'

Again he chuckled, but there was no humour in his light blue eyes. In spite of the warmth of the underground bunker the staff officers of the First Tank Army shivered and told themselves they would not like to be in the Fritzes' shoes on the morrow.

TWO

The advance to the village of Pokrovka was a walk-over – not much different from a pre-war road march, von Dodenburg couldn't help thinking – interrupted only by Popov dive-bombing attacks and occasional snipers. But the Stormaviks were rattled and inaccurate, and the heart seemed to have gone out of the snipers, usually the elite of the Red Army. They surrendered as soon as they had claimed their first unsuspecting victim and Wotan's special anti-sniper squad went into action, accepting their inevitable fate without much fight. Their camouflaged bodies, their faces painted a sickly light green, hung from the trees on both sides of the dusty white road, marking Wotan's advance.

The only real problem that morning was the heat, with the panzer grenadiers, forced to march because their half-tracks had been knocked out the previous day, dropping like flies. All along the route 'chain dogs' forced the scared peasants out with buckets of water for the foot-sloggers and they lapped it straight out of the pails like so many parched mongrels. In the end the Vulture sent a DR man [1] ahead of the column to warn each miserable, tumbledown Popov farm to be ready with water for his men, who were now beginning to fall out in the tremendous heat. In one place he even managed to find an antiquated Popov fire-engine and when the limping infantry staggered by, each panzer grenadier was sprayed from head to foot by the bare-footed Popov peasants working the handle as if their miserable lives depended upon it. But within a matter of minutes their black soaked uniforms were beginning to steam as the burning merciless sun dried them out.

In the tanks they had at least a faint breeze created by their movement, and in von Dodenburg's, in particular, Schulze's series of ribald stories about his pre-war life in Hamburg's great Free Port took their minds off the overwhelming heat.

'It was a good life in them days,' he recalled fondly over the intercom, 'before that shitty Lesbian talked me into this mob – me with an 'Old Un who thought the sun shone out of Thaelmann's arsehole! [2] 'Mind you, you had to pay for your pleasures – even then. I remember when I got my full house in 1938. [3] It was just before the Führer decided in his infinite wisdom that we needed a bit of Austrian scenery to make a Third Reich a more attractive place for Ami tourists—'

'Get on with it, Schulze,' von Dodenburg interrupted

1. Dispatch-rider, using a motorbike (transl.)
2. Thaelmann, head of the German Communist Party till 1933 (transl.)
3. Soldiers' slang for both venereal diseases.

hastily. He knew their intercom was monitored back at Corps and he didn't want Schulze getting in trouble with the Gestapo because of his malicious talk.

'Well, as I was saying,' Schulze continued without rancour. 'When I got my packet, the medics really give me a working over. Without as much as by-your-leave, they had me skivvies down and some sodding bone-mender was sticking his sausage finger up my rear end – right up. I thought he was trying to push through my guts to the other side.'

'You may laugh,' Schulze said. 'But it wasn't funny. There they were, five or six of them, Professor Doctor this and Doctor Doctor that looking at my joystick, as if it were going to come off in their hands the very moment. I can tell yer, it really put the wind up me. But that wasn't all. One of the bone-menders got this rod. It was as thick as one of Sergeant Metzger's butcher's fingers. Well he got hold of my love tube and—'

But Schulze was not fated to be able to relate the rest of his gory tale. Up ahead the Vulture's command Tiger, leading the column, skidded to a sudden stop, showering the plodding grenadiers on both sides with thick choking white dust. Tank after tank followed suit and it was a few moments before their crews could see the reason for their CO's hasty halt. But once the dust had cleared, the full horror of it was soon apparent. Two figures in blood-stained field-grey were hanging from what looked like shattered telegraph posts, their heads ringed with pieces of twisted barbed wire; and to complete the crucifixion, their 'dice-breakers' had been removed so that the retreating Ivans could stab at their naked feet with their bayonets as they hurried past.

Horrified the tankers and the panzer grenadiers crowded round the two poles, oblivious to the danger from snipers of the Stormoviks, and stared up at the two victims who wore the armbands of the *Grossdeutschland*.

'God in heaven,' someone broke the heavy silence, his voice at breaking point. 'Will you look at their flies!'

The crowd of suddenly white-faced men followed the direction of his shaking forefinger. Now they saw what he was pointing at.

'What a piggery!' Sergeant Metzger standing on the deck of the command tank roared, his stupid face crimson with rage and horror. 'The Popovs have cut the poor shits' eggs off!'

At the cry one of the two NCOs crucified on the poles raised his gory head slowly. A hush fell on the assembled troopers who stared at his ruined manhood in transfixed horror. He opened his eyes and croaked, 'Ivans – NKVD ... Caught us yesterday ... Commissar ordered.' He broke off, his dark eyes looking down at them, full of unbearable pain.

'Holy straw sack!' someone cried hotly. 'Did you hear that? The Popov police did that to them. Christ on crutch, don't let me get my paws on one of those bastards. I'll cut his communist eggs off with a broken beer bottle!'

'Yes, you're right, pal,' a half hundred voices cried. 'That's what the Ivan bastards deserve – their nuts sliced off slowly!'

'Get back to vehicles!' the Vulture's harsh incisive Prussian voice cut into the cries of rage and horror. 'I'll deal with this.'

The tankers swung round, their eyes narrowed against the white-hot sun, to stare up at the Vulture, his hand clasped on his Walther.

'But sir,' someone protested. 'What about those poor buggers up there?'

'Leave it to me. Now heaven, arse and twine, will you get

back to your tanks before the Popovs start knocking us as if we were on a shooting gallery!'

Hastily they fled back to their vehicles, while the Vulture drew his pistol and without appearing to take aim fired once. The NCO from the *Grossdeutschland* jerked convulsively. His gory head fell down. The Vulture thrust his Walther back in its holster.

'Sergeant Metzger,' he snapped, 'give them both a burst to make sure. Aim at their faces. I don't like the men following to see the crows pecking at their eyes.'

As the column started to move off again, Sergeant Metzger pressed the trigger of his schmeisser. A burst of 9 mm slugs ripped into the faces of the two crucified men from the *Grossdeutschland*. They disappeared at once. As the tanks rolled by, everyone looked studiously at the other side of the road, while the blood streamed down from the men's faces, drip-dripping into the white dry dust.

Thirty minutes later they took Pokrovka and the prisoners started to roll in, driven into the village by Schwarz's second Company coming from the left flank and von Dodenburg's First from the right. But this time Wotan's enraged troopers were not content with their usual mechanical execution of their Ivan POWs. They wanted the Popovs to suffer a long time just like the two men on the telegraph poles had suffered.

A group of shaken, filthy young eighteen-year-olds from a Moscow Guards Battalion were driven into the village's shabby onion-towered wooden church, whose peeling blue- and gold baroque ornaments looked as if they had not been painted since the days of the Czar. Then the place was set alight. As soon as the flame-throwing tank, which did the job, had backed off, the 2nd Company under Schwarz hurried forward to watch for any attempt to break out and gloat over the piteous cries for mercy and aid which came from the church as soon as the flames really began to take hold.

While the 2nd Company was thus occupied, a group from the 3rd drove a group of Siberians into the dusty white village square and set about them with their entrenching tools, cleaving their shaven skulls as if they were prime Soviet melons.

But worse was still to come. A party under Metzger was searching the wrecked village for diesel to replenish their half-empty tanks. As always in such cases they checked the place's collective farm first and it was there that they found the 'chain dog'.

His mutilated body had been tossed on a manure heap after they had finished with him. The hands had been hacked off, the eyes had gone too, but that was nothing to what the unknown torturers had done to the military policeman's anus. They had thrust the silver plate – which the 'chain dogs' wore round their necks and gave them their army nickname – up the orifice sideways, leaving the silver chain dangling purposelessly from it.

'Oh my God!' a young blond soldier next to Metzger gasped and before he could cover his mouth, the vomit started to shoot from between his lips in hot grunts and gasps.

The news flashed from soldier to soldier. Despite the Vulture's frantic attempt to maintain discipline, the men of the Wotan Battalion went wild. Running from cellar to cellar, they drove the civilians out screaming at them like crazy men, the froth bubbling at their lips. Who gave the order, no one ever discovered later. But the lime-caked boards covering the great cess-pool had been torn off and they were thrusting the civilians into the evil green-yellow mess. Men, women and children – they kicked them into it,

101

whacking them across their slimy heads when they refused to drown straight away. One old man with a great white Cossack moustache simply would not go under and half a dozen of them, screaming and cursing, beat his tough old wrinkled face into pulp before he finally sank below the stinking mess of faeces.

Then they discovered the Commissar hiding behind the sacks of grain in the barn at the back of the collective farm. Half a dozen dragged him out, his pudgy hands raised above his dark curly hair, clearly revealing the gold star of the political officer on his sleeve. 'Don't shoot . . . don't shoot,' he pleaded in a thick, but recognisable German.

'You're an Issy, aren't you?' someone yelled, the words in German finally penetrating his crazed brain, 'Come on – out with it!'

'No, no,' the fat fleshy Russian stammered hastily, as they pushed him towards the bubbling cesspool with the old man's hand still protruding from it. 'No, no, I learned it at school. At school, you understand?'

'Go on,' a dozen voices jeered. 'You're an Abie all right. Come on, you Ivan bastard – admit it!'

'Why don't yer take his breeches down,' someone suggested. 'They've all had their tails docked. Then you can tell.'

'Yeah, yeah,' they agreed. 'Get his breeches down.'

A dozen hands grabbed at his breeches and ripped them down. The Commissar's underpants – silk – followed. A second later he was standing there with pants hanging down over his well-polished, hand-made riding boots.

'Well,' a heavy-set corporal growled, 'let's see if he's an Issy. Come on, let's have a look at his shitty tail!'

A sweating panzer grenadier, one side of his face covered in blood, lifted up the struggling commissar's shirt with his bayonet. He whistled through his front teeth at what his move revealed. 'Look at that asparagus Tarzan,' he said. 'He's had his tail docked by the senior Issy all right . . . With a blunt razor blade by the looks of it.'

'No, no,' the Commissar yelled frantically, his German improving by the second. 'It was an operation! I had to have it done for medical reasons—' The heavy-set corporal slapped him hard across the face and the babble of protests stopped abruptly. 'Listen Issy, we know what you and your terrorists did to that chain dog. Chopped off his flippers. Peepers out and then if that ain't bad enough, you stick his badge up his arse.' He shook his head in bewilderment. 'How can you do things like that?'

'But it wasn't me!'

'Yeah, not you,' they sneered. 'Not now that we've got you with yer shitty knickers down. But it'd be diffcrent if you were getting a medal from Ehrenburg now, wouldn't it?' [1]

'But—'

Again the big corporal hit him across the face. The Commissar staggered back, spitting out blood and teeth, his dark eyes wide and staring with shock.

For a moment there was silence, broken only by the Russian's whimpering and the heavy enraged breathing of the circle of young flushed SS men all around him.

'All right, Issy,' the corporal said slowly and deliberately, as if he had just made up his mind. 'Now we're gonna make that little Jewish tail of yours a bit shorter still.'

'What – what,' the other man stuttered, not quite understanding the Army slang in German.

The query froze on his lips as the corporal brought out a penknife from his back pocket. It was the kind used by old

---

1. I. Ehrenburg, the Russian novelist, who was generally regarded by the common soldier in the German Army as being behind the hate propaganda directed against the Wehrmacht.

soldiers to chop up the issue plug tobacco they smoked in their little shag pipes. Almost casually he slipped open the blade and tested its sharpness with a practised thumb movement. The Commissar watched him in frozen terror.

'Get him on the ground,' the corporal said softly, all anger apparently gone from his voice. 'And hold him tight.'

A dozen hands threw the commissar to the dusty scuffed ground and held him there while he stared up at his torturer with dark eyes filled with fear and loathing. But now he did not attempt to protest any more. It was as if he had accepted his fate already.

The corporal bent over him with the knife and flapped back his shirt tail to reveal again the limp piece of dark flesh against the soft whiteness of the well-fed belly. He took a deep breath and prepared to cut. But another hand seized the knife.

'Give me that,' an authoritative voice snapped.

The corporal turned round, a curse on his lips. But it stayed there. Lieutenant Schwarz was staring down at the trapped Jew, murder in his dark eyes.

'This is going to be my job,' he said in a thick strange voice, not taking his gaze off their victim.

'Yessir – of course, sir,' the corporal said, backing away and touching his temple significantly to the others behind Schwarz's back. Schwarz fell to his knees in the thick white dust and ran his thumb along the blade of the penknife as the corporal had done, while the Russian stared up at him in silence.

His left hand shot out and seized the Russian's organ gingerly. He tensed. But still the prisoner made no sound. The fear had gone from his pale pudgy face now. It was replaced by hate – sheer naked hate. Schwarz licked his suddenly dry lips and took a firmer hold on the penknife. Suddenly the prisoner hawked and before Schwarz could dodge he had spat directly in the SS officer's dark face. *'German,'* the Commissar hissed, as if the name alone were a curse, *'German pig!'*

Schwarz swallowed. Without attempting to wipe away the dripping spittle, he started to saw.

Three hours later, SS Assault Battalion Wotan hit the second line of Soviet defence. It stopped them dead.

THREE

Against the blood-red disc of the setting sun, the Russian positions were outlined a stark menacing black, their every detail revealed.

'The Popovs must actually have found a general who can think further than his Party membership card,' the Vulture said thoughtfully, lowering his glasses and tugging at the end of his monstrous nose. 'Whoever he is, he's sited his positions very nicely – very nicely indeed.'

Von Dodenburg and Schwarz said nothing. There was no sound save the crackling of the flames still burning in the two Tigers hit that afternoon.

'I don't have to tell you gentlemen,' the Vulture continued, 'that the Popovs have got any attacker by the short hairs. That stream on the right flank there and the railway embankment on the left – the damn thing must be at least three metres high – would channel any attack into an area of, say, a kilometre. And as you can see, that kilometre is exceedingly well covered by their prepared positions, which are also located on the high ground.'

'Give me the order to advance, sir,' Schwarz said hotly,

his eyes gleaming crazily, 'and I'll cut through the Ivans with my Second like a dose of salts.'

The Vulture lowered his glasses and looked at him in mock sadness. 'My dear young Schwarz! You'd lose half your precious Second before you'd gone two hundred metres. Look at those Popov anti-tank guns dug in over there on the railway embankment. Once you had offered them your flank, they'd pick off your Tigers as if they were on the firing range. One after another.'

'So it's the back door then, sir,' von Dodenburg said wearily.

The Vulture nodded. 'Yes. A frontal attack would be suicidal and a flank attack is impossible.' He chuckled cynically. 'I had been expecting some act of God. After all the Popovs are atheists and we Germans are fighting a holy war out here. But the Almighty seems to have withdrawn his support of our cause of late. So the back door it will have to be.'

Von Dodenburg ignored his CO's cynicism. 'The embankment is out, sir. That leaves the river. We could cross it, put in an infantry attack and try to roll up the right flank. Combined with a flank attack by the rest of the Battalion at that point, we should probably pull it off.'

'Not should, my dear von Dodenburg, must!'

At his side, Schwarz clicked his heels together formally. 'I volunteer the Second for the mission, sir,' he rapped.

The Vulture shook his head. 'No, Schwarz, not you. But von Dodenburg here. What is left of his company after this afternoon is virtually infantry anyway and you've still got most of your Tigers. Von Dodenburg will do it and you will launch the flank attack.'

'But Sir—'

The Vulture ignored his protests, and in five minutes the attack was worked out in the tradition of the Armed SS, which had gained a reputation in Russia these last few years for swift if costly actions.

'Attack at zero three hundred hours as soon as you hear the diversionary attack on the embankment put in by the Third,' the Vulture concluded. 'And the best of luck von Dodenburg.'

'Thank you, sir.'

'Now I suggest you get some sleep before you attempt to get across that stream.'

But despite his weariness, there was no sleep for von Dodenburg that evening, nor for the rest of his Company. Instead he sat next to Schulze lazily watching the men heating cans of Old Man over the petrol fires, their faces hollowed out and made old and worn by the flickering blue flames. All was silent save for the low murmur of the troopers' conversation and the dry pistol cracks from Schwarz's lines. As usual the Second was shooting prisoners again. Schulze lit another of the long-stemmed black tobacco Russian cigarettes, exhaled a thin stream of evil-smelling smoke and coughed thickly. He pulled a wry face.

'Christ this *mahorka*,' he cursed softly. 'Makes yer mouth taste like a gorilla's armpit!'

Von Dodenburg laughed. 'Should be glad you've got them. Over in the Third they're down to smoking tea leaves in pieces torn from the *Schwarze Korps*.' [1]

'Ugh,' Schulze said. 'That'd be enough to put anybody off these cancer sticks for good.' But the usual broad grin was absent from his tough waterfront face.

'What's up, Schulze?' von Dodenburg asked. 'You're looking like the celebrated pregnant duck at the moment.'

Schulze did not answer immediately. Instead he stared at a trooper who was mixing a fresh mixture of dirt and petrol

1. The newspaper of the SS (transl.)

to the consistency of porridge before lighting it to heat another can of the Old Man.

'It's the future, sir,' he said at length, his face suddenly illuminated by the whoosh of the petrol stove igniting. 'I hate to sodding well think what it's gonna bring.'

'What do you mean?'

Schulze jerked his head in the direction of the Second's lines. 'That.'

'How?' von Dodenburg queried.

'We can't get away with that kind of shitty carry-on much longer sir.' He prodded the SS runes on his collar, sparkling in the blue light of the stove. 'Half the world these days is scared shitless as soon as they see these – even in the Reich. And the other half hates our guts so much that all they can think about is arranging for us to look at the potatoes from underneath. We've got too much blood on our hands – Belgium, France and now Popovland again. Everywhere the sods hate us.'

'But someone's got to do the job, Schulze,' von Dodenburg said seriously. The Reich is fighting for its survival and we're the Führer's Fire Brigade.'

'I know that, sir. I know that. But look what it's made of us. Those troopers who pushed the Popovs in the shit-pit this afternoon were still learning Schiller's crappy poetry at school six months ago – all full of nobility and the sodding German spirit. And that corp over there? He indicated the heavy-set NCO who had pulled the knife on the Soviet Commissar. 'A year ago when he first joined the mob, he used to cry himself to sleep because he thought he'd never make a soldier and because he missed his big-titted Mummy. Look at him now, a killer – a cold-hearted killer. Just like the rest of us.'

Von Dodenburg looked at Schulze hotly. 'We're not

killers, Sergeant Schulze. We are soldiers – the elite of the nation, the best Germany has.'

But Schulze was not impressed by von Dodenburg's attempt to pull rank. 'We're damned,' he said dourly. 'You and me, Wotan, the whole sodding SS – all of us, *we're damned.*'

A twig cracked underfoot.

'Watch yer sodding feet,' a dozen voices hissed angrily.

Cautiously von Dodenburg put his right foot into the dark swift-running stream. The current was strong but not too strong. 'Hold tight,' he whispered and moved in up to his waist. Behind him the men holding the rope tight around him took the strain.

'Here, give it me,' Schulze snapped and took hold of it. He was his usual businesslike self again. 'Some of you stupid bastards'd lose yer eggs if they weren't sewn up inside a sack, never mind this rope. All right sir, I've got it now. You can go ahead.'

Cautiously von Dodenburg began to wade his way across, his machine pistol held above his head. The current started to tug at his feet. Below them he could feel the smooth stones roll and slip. Suddenly the current took away his grip. Instantly Schulze held the strain. But von Dodenburg had been prepared for the effect of the current. With his right hand he began to strike out for the bushes fifty metres or so downstream, while Schulze and the rest played out the rope behind him. A few minutes later he was treading water and then clambering up the muddy bank, trying to make as little noise as possible.

Hurriedly he fixed the line and gave two rapid tugs on it to signal Schulze that he was across. Crouched in the bushes, machine pistol at the alert, he could hear the big NCO propelling himself across without the aid of the rope.

And he wasn't even breathing hard when he dropped at von Dodenburg's side, shaking the water off his pants and pulling on his tunic at the same time.

'Where are they, sir?' he asked softly.

'Can't you smell them?'

Schulze turned his head slightly to one side and sniffed the faint breeze. 'Yeah, I can now. The Ivans are pretty damn good at camouflaging themselves, but they can't hide that pong of theirs.'

Von Dodenburg nodded. There was an unmistakable odour about the Russian soldier – a compound of black tobacco, their hard yellow washing soap and the garlic sausage to which they were addicted – which always gave them away.

'Over there – fifty metres or more. At two o'clock.'

'That little hillock, sir?'

'Yes. That'll be it. They're dug in on the other side of it in their usual way with a look-out behind that central bush more than likely.'

For a moment or two they stared at the seemingly inno-cent rise; then Schulze whispered, 'What's the plan?'

In answer, von Dodenburg drew out the soldier's bayonet he had brought with him for this job. Its blade gleamed wickedly in the thin yellow light of summer moon which had just peered from behind the clouds.

'Get you, sir,' Schulze said hoarsely. 'I'll use my Reeper-bahn[2] equaliser.' Swiftly he slung his machine pistol and reaching in his pocket, slipped on a set of brass knuckles. He clenched his hamlike fist and spat on them for luck. 'They've knocked out more choppers, sir than you've had hot dinners.'

'No doubt, Schulze,' said von Dodenburg. 'But let's get

2. The notorious red light district of the great port (transl.)

110

the men over first before you start your disgraceful water-front tricks.'

'Yeah, before them mothers' darlings over there start pee-ing their pants with fear.'

Hastily they brought the rest of the company across and left them crouching in the bushes while Schulze and von Dodenburg advanced cautiously on the first Russian out-post, the only sound their tense breathing and the faint rustle of the yellow grass. As usual the Russian position was so well camouflaged that they had almost bumped into it before they noticed it. Suddenly von Dodenburg's heart gave a leap. A Popov was crouched right in front of him, the top half of his body clad in an earth-coloured smock. For one long moment they just stared at each other. Then the Popov's broad peasant face began to register the fact that the man crouching in the darkness five metres away was an enemy soldier. His mouth opened.

Von Dodenburg did not give him chance to shout. With a great leap he was on him. '*Not the helmet,*' his brain screamed at him. '*The bayonet will glance off! The throat!*' With a crash he hit the Popov. The bayonet bored deep into his neck. There was a sound like air rushing out of a sud-denly holed pipe. Together they tumbled to the bottom of the trench. He felt the Russian's body beginning to go limp beneath him. He dug the bayonet in again. Hot blood spurted over his knuckles and ran up his sleeve. Still the Russian did not die.

'Croak, you bastard!' he cursed vehemently and thrust the bayonet home once more.

The sentry's face contorted in agony. A clot of blood shot out of the side of his mouth. His head fell to one side. He was dead. For one long second, von Dodenburg felt abso-lutely exhausted, his mind an aimless blank. But gradually the sounds of a new danger penetrated his consciousness. He pulled out the blood-stained bayonet and scrambled like a lunatic out of the hole.

Two Popovs were running awkwardly at Schulze, great long bayonets pointed at his belly. Schulze did not move. He waited for them.

'*Move it!*' von Dodenburg screamed a warning, though he dare not say the words aloud.

When it seemed that the Russians would run Schulze through the guts, he acted. Swerving abruptly to one side, he kicked the first Popov in the crotch and launched a terrible punch at the second one. The first man went down screaming horribly. The other's false teeth – a stainless steel set, which gleamed in the moonlight – bulged suddenly out of his mouth.

'Stop that bastard screaming,' Schulze ordered and threw himself on the second man.

Von Dodenburg dived on the Russian writhing on the ground, the vomit spurting up from between his teeth clenched in agony. With one swift movement he drew the razor-sharp bayonet across his exposed throat. For what seemed an age nothing happened. Then, a thick red line appeared along the whole length of the stricken Russian's neck. Von Dodenburg pressed his hand across the man's mouth to prevent him screaming and did it again.

Above him Schulze drew back his fist and smashed it into the other Popov's face. Von Dodenburg could hear his nose-bone snap like a dry twig. Blood spurted out of his smashed nose. Still he did not go down. Schulze hit him again. The Russian's right eye disappeared in a mass of thick blood. But although he was now swaying badly like a very drunken man, he still remained on his feet.

'Go down you shitty Popov bastard,' Schulze cursed sotto voce. 'Do you want to die a sodding hero's death or something?'

The Russian muttered something, blood pouring from his terribly mutilated face. While the man on the ground died, von Dodenburg's hand pressed over his mouth so that he wouldn't scream, the young officer watched as Schulze prepared to hit the wildly swaying Russian again.

'Right you brave sod!' Schulze hissed. 'Take that!' With all his enormous strength he crashed his metal fist right into the centre of the Russian's brow.

The Popov shot backwards to hit the ground three metres away. Schulze did not give him a chance to get up again. He threw himself forward. His big hob-nailed 'dice-breaker' crashed down on the man's ruined face. Once, twice. Von Dodenburg could hear the facial bones splinter and crack. Still the Russian tried to get up.

'Christ on a crutch, man!' Schulze cried beside himself with rage and despair. 'Do you soddingly well want to live for ever?' With the last of his strength he launched one final kick at the Russian. It caught him at the point of his shattered jaw. His scream of agony died abruptly under the impact of that tremendous blow. His head shot back. Something snapped and he was dead before his head hit the ground.

Five minutes later the storm broke. First there was thunder, as bad as a heavy bombardment with air support from Stukas. Lightning ripped the darkness apart. Then it came down in torrents. Enormous drops started pattering against their steel helmets. Hastily the troopers pulled their camouflaged capes about them and started to plod forward. The ground turned into a thick red mire almost immediately, but it had the advantage of muffling any sound they made as they began to advance towards the main Soviet positions, guided by the agreed-upon signal flares fired from their own lines. Doggedly they slogged their way through the quag-

113

mire, the young officer and Schulze in the lead, their machine pistols held at the alert.

'Holy straw sack,' some young soldier mumbled just behind von Dodenburg, 'just think of being at home in a warm clean bed tonight and able to sleep the clock round—'

'Twice,' someone else said next to him, 'At least twice.'

'Yeah, and then good bean coffee and hot rolls.'

'With apricot jam. You've got to have apricot jam with hot rolls.'

'And what about a little bit of soft titty too?' Schulze's voice butted into their reverie. 'Knock it off, you silly young sods! What do you think this is – a shitty girls' school's outing or something!'

Von Dodenburg smiled thinly to himself in spite of the raindrops trickling down the inside of his jacket. Trust old Schulze for bringing even the greatest dreamer down to earth with a crash. Suddenly an urgent foreign-sounding voice called through the dripping darkness.

'Over here, Fritz – Fritz, can't you hear me?'

The smile vanished from von Dodenburg's wet face. He froze. Behind him in the pouring rain the company came to a ragged halt.

'Nobody move – nobody answer!' Schulze hissed at his side. Carefully he began to raise his Schmeisser, peering into the darkness.

'Fritz – over here,' the strange disembodied voice called again. 'What's wrong with you Fritz, can't you hear me?'

'Down,' von Dodenburg commanded in a tense voice.

The strange voices came from all sides now. 'Fritz here ... Fritz, what's wrong ... Fritz.'

But the old hands knew the Popov trick. The veterans among them clapped their dirty, muddy paws over the mouths of the recruits to prevent them calling out. A single shot rang out from somewhere to the left. It echoed hollowly

114

through the rain. An age seemed to pass while they searched in vain through the darkness for the enemy. Another shot rang out.

And another, from a different direction.

It was a nerve-racking business and von Dodenburg, hugging the mud with the length of his soaked body, breathed a silent prayer of thanks that not one of his men had fired back and betrayed their position. The Popovs were just as puzzled as they were. The sniping continued for some time. Twice slugs sliced the air just above their heads, and once the firing seemed to come from somewhere behind them. Then it stopped as abruptly as it had started, leaving behind an echoing silence.

'*Standfast*,' von Dodenburg hissed. He knew that this was the worst test of all. If their nerves broke now and they started to move – either forward or backwards – the Popovs would annihilate them. But the First Company held steady.

The minutes passed leadenly. Then they heard a soft movement up ahead to their left. The Popovs came as silently as they could. Their boots would be off and any part of their equipment which might clink would be muffled in rags or removed. But they were coming all right.

Von Dodenburg nudged Schulze. 'Can you hear them?'

'Yes! I'll pass the word.'

Hastily the alarm ran from mouth to mouth, as the faint sounds grew louder. There seemed a lot of them, and now von Dodenburg could hear them slipping in the mud of the slight incline immediately ahead of them. Carefully he pulled out his only incendiary grenade.

A dark hesitant shape loomed up ten metres away. And another. By the very way they stood, he guessed they did not realise how close they were to the German positions. The first man raised his hand, as if signalling to the rest to

115

follow him. Other dark squat shapes appeared out of the streaming rain.

'*Now!*' von Dodenburg screamed and hurled the grenade at the first shape.

It exploded instantly. A fierce spurt of bright white flame shot up the Ivan's body. A wildly contorted, terrified face came into view, and disappeared screaming in the flames. The next instant the vicious volley hit the Russian line. A dozen of them were bowled over, yelling with the shock of it.

And then they were charging the Germans. Almost at once the muddy field became a bloody chaos, with little groups of cursing, screaming men stabbing, shooting, clawing each other in the red morass, skidding from side to side like ice skaters. 'Christ, he's stabbed in the guts . . . I'm stabbed . . . Stretcher-bearer . . . I'm shot . . . The sodding bastards have shot me . . .' The frenzied frightened agonized cries rose on all sides in Russian and German.

An enormous Ivan, stinking of garlic and black tobacco launched himself at von Dodenburg. The officer let him have a burst in the guts. He flew backwards and sat down in the mud. Von Dodenburg jammed his butt in the man's face. Something snapped and the man toppled backwards. Another trooper stepped on his face, pressing it deep into the mud. An Ivan loomed up out of the streaming rain. He clutched a round-barrelled tommy gun to his side. But von Dodenburg fired first. His arms fanned the air as he fell over, gurgling horribly through his punctured wind pipe.

Then 1st Company's only flame-thrower hissed into action. A long tongue of flame licked the Ivans' front rank. A squat officer with enormous epaulettes screamed as his body went up in flames. The terrible weapon cut the night again. A young Popov was engulfed by the stream of fire. Screaming hideously he rolled down the other side of the slope, his arms and legs flailing madly in his immense agony.

Another followed him like a human catherine wheel. And another. Panic broke out. The Popovs started to throw away their weapons, clawing at each other to get out of the way of that monstrous flame.

And they had burst through them and were running madly across the soaking steppe into the darkness. By the time the urgent Popov signal flares had begun to hiss into the sky to be followed by the first howls of the Stalin organs on the position they had just held, the survivors of the 1st Company had vanished into the streaming rain, leaving only their dead and dying behind them.

FOUR

Like grey Russian timber wolves they sneaked out of the shattered fir forest towards the unsuspecting Popovs. It was now nearly three, time for the diversion. Behind them the angry Russian mortar stonk had died down. It had given way to short nervous bursts of machine gun fire, as if the Russian gunners still thought they were out there somewhere on the soaking steppe.

Von Dodenburg crouched and gave a hand signal. A couple of the veterans hushed forward, unarmed save for the trench knives clasped in their big muddy fists. The Popov sentries did not even move as they tugged back their helmets, pulled hard at the straps to strangle their first surprised cries of alarm and slid the razor-sharp knives between their ribs.

Von Dodenburg signalled again. Bent and at the double, they advanced on the stark outline of M-13 rocket-launchers, which guarded the rear of the Popov positions. A sentry staggered half asleep from between two huge piles of 30 mm rockets. Schulze hit him with the Reeperbahn equalizer. He went down as if he had been pole-axed, the bloody ruin of his mouth full of broken teeth.

'Grenades,' von Dodenburg whispered urgently as they crouched next to the unconscious sentry.

A bareheaded giant with two huge sacks of grenades, in addition to the three belts of Spandau ammo slung over his enormous chest, dropped into the mud beside him.

'The cannon,' said von Dodenburg. 'Time fuse for –' he checked the luminous dial of his issue watch '– exactly five minutes from now.'

The gigantic grenadier disappeared into the rain. Von Dodenburg put his hand on the centre of his helmet, the signal for 'to me.'

The twenty or so survivors of the 1st Company crowded around him, the raindrops dripping off the rims of their helmets.

'Break up into twos. Check that you've all got grenades. Post yourselves outside the bunkers.' He indicated the squat outlines of the dug-in Russian positions below the mortar battery. 'As soon as the white flares start coming up from the south-east, you know that the balloon's going up. Then in, double quick and sort the Popovs out. No messing. Grenade through the opening and straight on inside.'

'Prisoners?' somebody asked softly.

'Nix! We've got no time for them. Besides we haven't enough men spare to guard them. No, clean the Popovs out and then get yourselves ready for their counter-attack. The whole idea is to hold this position until Lieutenant Schwarz's 2nd Company can reach us. Any questions now?' He stared round their pale blobs of faces under the dripping helmets. 'All right, Schulze, you come with me. The rest of you – happy landings!'

'Happy landings, sir,' they answered dutifully.

Swiftly they stole away and posted themselves at the entrances of the Russian bunkers, fingers tensed on their weapons. There was no sound save the snoring of their unsuspecting victims inside and the rat-tat of some ancient Russian machine gun a long way off, chopping away like some dogged woodpecker. Von Dodenburg looked at the luminous dial of his watch. Still two minutes to go. Time seemed to have stopped. He felt the sweat begin to start up all over his body. He freed one hand and then the other from his machine pistol and wiped them dry on his trousers. It was tension that was making him sweat, he knew that. It was always the same at moments like this. He gripped his Schmeisser again and within seconds his hands were slimy with perspiration again. He cursed softly to himself and released his right hand. Suddenly there was a hush. He turned, startled. A flare had sailed into the air, and another. Schulze's big face suddenly shone an unnatural white. For a moment the young officer did not move. He couldn't. He seemed rooted to the spot. Another flare hissed into the dripping sky. The Popov machine gunner quickened his fire. Below them in the bunker, the others began to stir uneasily.

'Now!' he roared suddenly.

Schulze shot forward. With his big boot, he kicked open the door of the bunker. In the same instant, he flung in the stick grenade and slammed the door shut again.

There was a thick muffled crump. A scream rang out. Schulze kicked open the door again and jumped back. Standing splay-legged in the opening, machine pistol tucked into his hip, von Dodenburg poured in a vicious hail of fire. He couldn't miss. The screaming half-dressed Popovs were packed in the entrance, clawing each other frantically in their efforts to get out. A couple of them, bleeding from multiple wounds, their faces blackened from the grenade explosion, staggered out, crying the only German word they knew, 'Comrade . . . comrade!'

Schulze did not hesitate. He kicked the two of them into the mud and stabbed them to death there in the crimson slush. Von Dodenburg rushed inside, his machine pistol held at the ready. The place stank of unwashed bodies and black tobacco which even the acrid smell of the explosive could not hide. He sprang over shattered bodies, illuminated by the hissing petroleum lamp still functioning on the little wooden table in the centre of the bunker. Suddenly he heard a faint whimpering. He spun round, his nerves going like trip hammers. To his right there was a dark passage leading off the main bunker. Pulling out his last remaining grenade, he ripped out the pin and lobbed it down the dark passage. Quickly he flung himself against the protection of the earth wall. At his feet a Popov groaned and tried to raise himself. As the grenade exploded he kicked the Russian viciously in the face. His head clicked back like that of a wooden puppet, his neck broken neatly.

Von Dodenburg sprang forward, spraying the passage with lead as he ran up it. But it was a waste of precious metal. The only occupants of the big inner chamber, which was obviously a command post, were already dead or dying. One sole Popov, whose stiff board epaulettes bore the golden insignia of a senior colonel, tried to raise himself, a red jet pumping from a severed artery in his throat. Von Dodenburg didn't give him a chance. The Russian fell back, his upper body shattered. Then there was no sound, save for an echoing silence and the soft dribble of the dying Colonel's blood into the dry dust.

Von Dodenburg staggered back against the wall and leaned there, his chest heaving frantically. They'd pulled it off; they'd done it! He felt all energy drain out of him, as if someone had just opened a secret tap. It seemed, as if he would never be able to move again. But a moment later, Schulze came running up the passage, crying out his name in alarm and in the far distance the German heavies opened up to support Wotan's attack. He pulled himself together.

'Here, Schulze,' he cried. 'I'm here.' Just as Schulze burst into the command post, the first Popov counter-fire hissed viciously over their heads, shaking the whole bunker and von Dodenburg knew the fun and games had started.

The whole line trembled like a dying animal. Time and time the rockets crashed down on it, their angry red tails streaking after them, as the Russians tried to knock out what was left of von Dodenburg's company. But the Popovs who had built the positions had done a fine job, as they always did, and although the bunkers rocked alarmingly, nothing but a direct hit could put them out of action. As Schulze roared between salvoes:

'I think I'll stay here for the duration, sir. It's safer!'

Von Dodenburg cupped his hands round his mouth, his teeth gleaming against his blackened face, and yelled back. 'Rather you than me, Schulze! It's like being in a force twelve gale – my stomach's heaving as if I'm on the high seas!'

But just after Schwarz's first attempt to break through to them failed, the artillery fire slackened and the infantry came in: masses of small men in earth-coloured blouses running forward in packed ranks, crying their usual hurrah. They mowed them down by the hundred, each two-man team working independently, confident of their superiority to these sub-human creatures who sacrificed their precious lives so frivolously. The Popov bodies piled up five deep only twenty metres from their positions, but they stopped them all right; and soon the survivors were streaming back the way they had come, leaving the battlefield to the artillery once more.

Soon the command bunker began to rock once more to the explosion of the rockets and what von Dodenburg took to be 105 mm guns. But now he had recovered his nerve. Peering through the loop-hole at the body-littered battlefield, he yelled:

'Schulze, I'll stand watch, while you go and see if you can rustle up anything to eat. The cabbage steam is beginning to rise within me.'

'Sir,' Schulze said, slinging the two Russian sub-machine guns he was using now that he had run out of ammunition for his own Schmeisser. 'But I can't promise you much except that boiled mongrel sausage the Ivans eat.'

'It sounds like the best Kempinski could provide,' von Dodenburg yelled, as Schulze, the born looter, began to rummage among the debris of the command bunker. But the big Hamburger returned with something else beside two hunks of coarse Popov black bread and wedges of bright red sausage balanced on them to be washed down with a fiery mixture of rain water and vodka.

He swallowed a piece of the garlic sausage and casually rolled a coin across the floor to where von Dodenburg squatted with his back against the trembling earth wall. Curiously the officer, his mouth full of bread and vodka mixture, picked it up and examined it.

'What is it?' he asked after a while. Schulze's reply was drowned by a fresh salvo of rockets. Impatiently he waited till they were finished, while von Dodenburg stared at the dull yellow coin with the Imperial Eagle of Old Russia stamped on one side and the head of an unidentifiable Czar on the other.

'Twenty rouble piece,' Schulze yelled finally.

'Oh,' the officer answered without too much interest, and was about to roll it across the floor back to Schulze when the Hamburger added:

'In gold – almost pure gold.'

Von Dodenburg whistled through his teeth, while Schulze observed his expression, a curious look in his usually frank eyes. 'Gold, eh?'

'Yeah, there's enough there to pay the great whore of Buxtehude for a whole week of nooky.'

'Is that so?'

'Hm, hm.' Schulze took another slug of vodka mixture and wiped the back of his sleeve across his mouth, but he did not take his eyes off von Dodenburg's face.

'All right, Schulze,' von Dodenburg bellowed as the Stalin organs started up again, 'Pee or get off the pot. You've got to tell something – good, tell me it.'

'Back in that other room, we must have killed a real old Russki big shot with that grenade. There wasn't much left of his upper body, but he had enough tin on his chest to make even our beloved CO envious as far as I could make out, his badges of rank made him out to be a major-general.'

'Any documents, maps and the like?' von Dodenburg roared.

'I didn't look, Captain. I found this – and that was enough for Mrs Schulze's little boy.' He reached inside his tattered, mud-stained tunic and brought out what looked like an old-fashioned money belt. He tossed it towards the officer and it fell heavily into the dust before him. 'If you want to count it,' he said. 'And I did – you'll find there are close on three hundred of them in there.'

'Well, you could have a lot of Buxtehude whores for that, Schulze.'

'I could, sir, but I don't want the whores. I've still got my good looks and my charm, sir after all. I don't need to buy my tail yet.'

'What do you want then?' von Dodenburg tensed as a 105 mm shell landed close behind the bunker, showering

123

earth and pebbles on their helmets. 'Well, go on – what do you want, man?'

'Out,' Schulze snapped laconically, his voice full of determination.

'Out of what.'

'Out of this shit, out of the Wotan, out of the SS, out of Germany!'

Von Dodenburg looked at him, his mouth open. 'What did you say?'

'You heard me, *Herr* von Dodenburg! But don't get me wrong. If some sodding Popov knocked me off tomorrow with a nice clean bullet, I wouldn't exactly welcome the event, but I'm not scared of it. What I'm scared shitless about is what is to come. I couldn't stand a Popov camp or any other POW cage. No booze, no dames – no, that's not for me.' He shook his head firmly. 'And that Marie there in the belt is our way out.'

'Our?' von Dodenburg echoed the word stupidly.

'Yeah, I want you to come along with me.' Eagerly Schulze explained his plan. How a couple of the coins would buy them a fake evacuation ticket on one of the hospital trains bound for the Reich. There he knew a man down at the docks – 'the little bastard's been inside the nick a couple of times and he likes his sauce, but he's the best forger in St Pauli' – who would fake them a couple of civilian ID cards. With these they would make their way into Occupied France and make contact with the Catalan professional smugglers who regularly took refugees across the frontier into Spain.

'From there, well,' Schulze shrugged expansively while von Dodenburg stared at him in open-mouthed disbelief, 'the world's ours – the Argentine, Brazil, Chile – who cares. As long as there's no war and no SS there.' He broke off suddenly. 'Well, what do you think, Herr von Dodenburg?

It's the only damn way to save our hides before it's too late!'

Von Dodenburg opened and closed his mouth rapidly like a stranded fish gasping for air. 'You, you,' he stuttered, unable to find the words to express his outrage. 'You can't expect me to—'

But he never completed the sentence. The roar of the Stalin organs stopped abruptly to be replaced by the rusty rattle of Tiger tracks. Outside a well-remembered Prussian voice rasped:

'Wotan to me – SS Assault Battalion Wotan rally on me!'
The Battalion had finally broken through.

FIVE

The bloody advance to Kursk went on under the merciless white-hot Russian sun. One day after they had broken through the second line of defence, a fleet of old three-engined 'Auntie Jus'[1] flew over their positions. Sedately and in perfect formation, despite the Russian flak, they released the great Do 230 gliders they had been towing. Moments later the gliders' monstrous black shadows zoomed in low over the baked steppe to make perfect landings. Before the Russian artillery ranged in on them, the glider pilots evacuated the wood and fabric planes, lying on the ground now like helpless birds.

Men and material poured from them. For the most part they were teenagers straight from the training schools, some of them with only six weeks' basic training behind them. Many of them, too, spoke German with outlandish accents

1. German army slang for the Junkers 52nd transport plane (transl.)

– ethnic Germans from all over occupied Europe, recruited by Reichsführer Himmler's 'body-snatchers' by force or false promises. The material wasn't much better either: patched-up Mark IVs from previous campaigns, armed with outdated short 75 mms, which hadn't been even properly fired in.

But in spite of Sergeant Metzger's disgruntled report to his CO that 'two hundred booty Germans and eight toy tanks' were 'present and correct', the Vulture was glad to have them. In the last four days the Battalion had lost nearly 50 per cent of its effectives and the new blood was urgently needed.

Twelve hours later, the Third Company, where most of the reinforcements went, was probing the Popov's third line of defence when it swung into a carefully staged Russian trap. Tempted into attacking what looked like a wandering Cossack cavalry battalion, the Third was flanked by a whole brigade of Soviet assault guns, cunningly dug-in hull-down on the high ground to their right. The Popov SU-76s were armed with the inferor 76 mm gun. Under different circumstances the 3rd Company's 88 mm would have made short work of them. But the SU-76s were so well dug in that they could blast one Tiger after another without a single casualty to themselves. Within thirty minutes the 3rd had ceased to exist. Only two German tanks escaped, one of them commanded by the 3rd's 20-year-old Commanding Officer.

He reported the loss of his company to the Vulture in the prescribed military way, then he excused himself for a moment and walked across to the nearest shattered tree, as if he were going to urinate. Instead he pulled out his duty pistol, placed it against his temple and squeezed the trigger. The bullet shattered his skull, the blood splattering the Vulture's over large riding boots. Calmly the Vulture took out

126

his handkerchief and flicked the blood off while an ashen-faced Metzger stared at him aghast.

'Bury the bloody fool, Metzger,' the Vulture rasped, no trace of emotion in his thin Prussian voice, 'and see that I sign the recommendation for a bit of tin for him – say, the Iron Cross, second class!' He sniffed and peered through his monocle to check if his boots were clean. 'That's about all he deserves for losing useless company like that. If this had been 1940 I would have court-martialled him. All right, Metzger, get the lead out of your arse! Move it!'

That same night a long line of trucks from the 8th Panzer Division which was in reserve rolled into their laager. A bewildered company of tankers in their black uniforms dropped into the dust and lined up in front of Geier and his officers. Hurriedly a heavy-set tank captain clicked to attention in front of the Vulture and made his report.

'Captain Stuke, 1st Company, Seventh Battalion and two hundred men, sir!'

The Vulture eyed him with a mirthless smile. Von Dodenburg knew what he was thinking – the Panzer Captain was a typical base stallion, his sole decoration the sport medal in bronze. Finally the Vulture returned the Captain's salute. -

'Welcome to SS Assault Battalion Wotan, Stuke,' he said.

'SS Assault Battalion Wotan!' the other officer echoed his words stupidly. 'But Major, no one told us at HQ that we were to join the Armed SS.'

'Well, this must be a pleasant surprise for you, eh! It isn't every day that one gets the opportunity to join an elite formation like the Wotan, is it?'

'Yes, yes, I understand that, Major,' Stuke said, his face growing red. 'But one needs time to make a decision like that. You'll forgive me, Major, but I can't simply join the Armed SS—'

'Do you or don't you?' the Vulture cut in icily, the smile

gone, his pale blue eyes gleaming dangerously. At his side von Dodenburg felt sorry for the blustering tank captain.

'No,' the other officer said lamely.

'Thank you, soldier,' the Vulture snapped and in the same instant he reached out and ripped off first one and then the other of the tanker's epaulettes. 'SS Soldier Stuke you may join the ranks.'

'But, this . . . this is an outrage,' the other man spluttered.

The Vulture ignored him completely. He turned to Officer Cadet Barsch, a one-armed veteran of the old Wotan, who had volunteered again for the Armed SS after being invalided out after losing his arm in 1941. Barsch's chest glittered with decorations for bravery. 'Barsch, will you be so kind as to take over the 3rd Company. Ensure that every man has the Wotan arm-band sewn on before dawn.'

'*Sir!*' Barsch yelled at the top of his voice, as if he were back on the parade ground at Bad Toelz. Pushing past the broken Panzer Captain, he bellowed at the new recruits. 'Welcome to the Wotan! All right, follow me – *at the double*!'

As the black-uniformed tankers stumbled after him, laden down with their kit, the newly demoted Captain in the rear, the Vulture turned to von Dodenburg and said: 'A word in your ear. Let the 3rd take the point – as long as they last. Barsch is a fool, but a brave one. He won't object. I need the old reliables for the real battle.'

'Real battle, sir?'

'Division heard from Gehlen's office this morning. The Popovs are holding the bulk of their armour near Kursk. They haven't flung in half their stuff yet. I need my old reliables for the day when they do. Up to now the Popovs have just been playing with us.'

Behind them Schulze groaned softly. 'If this is the first act,' he muttered, 'I'd hate to see the fucking second one . . .'

On the morning of July 9th, the Battalion was suddenly pulled out of the line, and hurried eight kilometres to the rear to 'receive an important personage', as the telephone order from Dietrich's HQ had it.

The important personage turned out to be Reichsführer Himmler himself, his skinny frame clad in the field-grey of a general in the Armed SS, his hollow chest decorated with the sports medal in bronze, Iron Cross third class and what looked like the Party's Blood Order. As he stepped out of his Storch, followed by a tubby brown-clad figure who looked like a middle-weight boxer gone to seed, Schulze, standing behind von Dodenburg said sotto voce:

'Do you think he'll get the Knight's Cross out of this visit? They tell me he's got throatache.'

'Shut up, Schulze,' von Dodenburg snapped without turning his head, 'Or I'll see you get arse-ache – damned quick, too!'

'SS Assault Battalion Wotan – *attention*!' Major Geier's voice rang out.

The Battalion snapped to attention. Stiffly the Vulture strode forward, halted the regulation six paces before the Reichsführer and the little burly Golden Pheasant, both dwarfed by the immaculate SS aides, some of whom were nearly two metres tall, and bellowed.

'SS Assault Battalion Wotan – four hundred men, eighteen officers, one officer-cadet – all present and correct, Reichsführer!'

Heinrich Himmler touched his pale, effeminate hand to his cap and smiled thinly: 'Thank you, my dear Geier. Good to see you again – and by the way, you've got your lieutenant-colonel stars. I approved them yesterday.'

The Vulture's face flushed with genuine pleasure. Promotion was the only thing that meant anything to him, apart from the beautiful powdered youths who frequented the Lehrter Station in Berlin after dark.

'Thank you, Reichsführer,' he barked, 'I am sure the Battalion will be pleased at the honour.'

The Reichsführer gave the Battalion a very careful inspection, behaving more like a sergeant-major than a commanding general, inspecting their tattered uniforms and dirty battle-damaged weapons as if they were back in peacetime Berlin and not in the heart of war-torn Russia. As Schulze sighed afterwards:

'He got up so close to have a gander at my throatache' – he meant his Knight's Cross – 'that I got more than enough of his sodding breath. God Almighty, it was so bad I'm surprised it didn't melt the flaming medal!'

But in the end the Reichsführer, who because he had been too young to see active service in World War One took his present military duties as the head of the Armed SS exceedingly serious, was satisfied. They were stood at ease while the Reichsführer attempted to clamber up the steep sides of a Tiger in order to address them. Twice he failed and waved aside the aides who rushed forward to help him while the fat Golden Pheasant grinned at his discomforture. But his spindly legs were not equal to the task and with an angry sigh, he beckoned to one of his gigantic aides to assist him.

Angrily he tugged at his tunic and faced them. 'Men of Wotan – comrades,' he began. 'It gives me great pleasure to be able to speak to you today. I am also sad at the same time to see how thin your ranks have become. But that is the sad privilege of your elite battalion – to be at the forefront of any attack for Folk, Fatherland and Führer.'

'Watch it, Heini,' Schulze cracked to his neighbour. 'You're going to rupture yourself if you go on like that!'

All around him the wooden-faced SS troopers tittered sud-

tered suddenly. But on the tank Himmler was too busy trying to get his breath back while the gigantic aide proferred
him a glass of his favourite lemonade. He only touched
alcohol on special occasions; his stomach was too delicate.

'But your sacrifices, comrades, have not been in vain. As
you know, we are pushing back the Bolshevik beast steadily
and inexorably. We are winning – definitely winning! Now
you, as the point of the Führer's own Bodyguard, have been
given the honour of delivering the death blow to the Soviet
beast.' He paused dramatically, his sickly face flushed a
sudden hectic red.

'In forty-eight hours at the latest,' Himmler continued,
'you as the point will hit the Soviet's fourth and major line
of defence. There the Soviets will have to stand and fight, or
run away for ever. They will stand, according to our Intelligence. Thus it will be your honour to give the first blows of
that tremendous battle.' He paused to get his breath and in
the front rank von Dodenburg could hear the air wheezing
through his diseased lungs.

Down below, the Golden Pheasant looked at his watch
and yawned in boredom, not even attempting to cover his
mouth with his fat hand. Idly von Dodenburg wondered
who he was, daring to affront Himmler in such a manner.

'Comrades, I cannot tell you very much. As you can
realise what knowledge I have is highly secret. But this much
I can say – the battle you will join in forty-eight hours' time
will be the greatest tank battle in all history, and when you
have fought it, those of you who survive will count it as the
most significant event in your whole lives.' His face cracked
into a wintery smile. 'And now comrades, before I and Folk
Comrade Bormann here leave,' he nodded his head at the
Golden Pheasant, whose broad face was beginning to
brighten now at the smell of the food, we should deem it an
honour if you would join us for a simple soldier's lunch.'

As the cooks began to plant the great tureens of steaming pea soup and sausage on the trestle tables set out behind the parade, the new Lieutenant-Colonel Geier bellowed: *'Sieg Heil!'* In his enthusiasm at his new promotion, he forgot his usual cynical distaste of the whole National Socialist theatricality.

'Sieg Heil!' the great cry rose from four hundred throats with a fervour that von Dodenburg, his face flushed an enthusiastic red as he stood there rigidly to attention, had not heard for a long, long time. Suddenly he felt confident again. The doubts cast by Sergeant Schulze vanished. They must beat the Popovs – they would.

'Sieg Heil!' he screamed, his eyes gleaming fanatically. *'Sieg Heil . . .'*

Metzger was given the job of picking the waiters to serve Himmler's table. A handful of men were delegated to report to him and Schulze, who as the only other rank with the Knight's Cross was to be in charge, went down their ranks quickly, selecting the ones he needed.

'You,' he snapped to a lanky youth from Rumania, 'say – can I give you the salt, Reichsführer.' He groaned when the boy repeated the phrase in barely understandable German. 'Get out of it, you shitty booty German, you!' he bellowed. 'What the hell do you think this battalion is – the crappy Foreign Legion!'

A couple of others were turned down because they weren't blond – it was well known that the Reichsführer only liked blond SS men around him although he was sallow and dark enough himself. Metzger looked at the tall soldier at the end of the line who had just joined them from the 8th Panzer.

'You'll do,' he said. 'But get that black jacket off – you're in the SS now, remember.'

The soldier's tough face cracked into a lazy grin. 'Who could forget, sergeant?' he said impudently. 'Pea soup and half a sausage with the Reichsführer one day – and a wooden overcoat the next! You certainly see life in the SS,'

'Button up your thick lip, you asparagus Tarzan you!' Metzger said threateningly, but he had no time to 'make a sow' out of the man as he would have done normally; the Reichsführer wanted some more mineral water and the kitchen bulls couldn't find any more. 'Schulze,' he said hurriedly, 'check their sausage fingers and see their nails haven't got half the steppe under them. Here, use this.'

He picked up the Russian bayonet which the cooks had been using to chop up the sausages for Himmler's table and throwing it to Schulze, hurried away to find some more soda water. Schulze passed it swiftly down the line, giving it to each man in turn to clean his nails. He came level with the soldier from the Eighth.

'All right, asparagus Tarzan, let's see your pinkies!' Schulze stared at his left hand. On each finger he had a dark blue letter tattooed. 'M-A-R-CH-E,' he read out aloud. 'Marche? What the hell does that mean?'

The big man held up his right hand. Each finger had a letter tattooed on it too.

'*Marche ou crève*, it says. It's French – and in case, you ain't cultured as I am, Sergeant, that's frog for march or croak.'

Schulze looked at him keenly. 'You in the Legion?'

'Sure, Sergeant,' the other man said easily. 'Eight years. I deserted in North Africa in 1941 as soon as the Afrika Korps landed in Libya and made my way across the frontier.'

'North Africa, eh,' Schulze said thoughtfully. 'I'd like to have a talk with you, my lad.'

'Any time, Sergeant. But don't expect me to fall in love

133

with you straight away. You see,' the ex-legionnaire gave him a mock simper, 'I left my one true love back in Africa.'

Sergeant Schulze made an obscene gesture, but all the same he was not displeased with the new recruit from the 8th; a vague plan was beginning to form in his mind.

Folk Comrade Bormann ate his first half litre of pea soup greedily, concentrating on eating, as if it had been a long time since he had last eaten, completely ignoring Himmler, his staff and Wotan officers all around him. Then he speared his half sausage and ate it the way the peasants do from the fork, letting the grease run down his pugnacious chin. That finished he belched, wiped his chin and broke into the conversation brusquely.

'I'm a Mecklenburger, you know.' His voice was coarse and harsh, and the assembled officers looked across at him startled. 'A thousand years ago, the Slavs lived there until we Germans kicked them out. Since then generations of good German peasants have toiled to make Mecklenburg and what lies east of it German – generation after generation of simple good German folk.' He raised his voice, which in spite of its coarseness was full of authority, as though Bormann were used to giving orders and expected them to be obeyed. 'Now if we don't beat the Bolsheviks this July, they will start pushing us back out of Russia. And they won't stop in Poland, nor in East Prussia. No, gentlemen, their target will be the Elbe, once the boundary of the ancient Slavic kingdom. Then Mecklenburg will be Slav again. That is why the battle you will be soon fighting, gentlemen, is so vital for the future of the Reich. It is as simple as that.'

There was a moment of awkward silence while Folk Comrade Bormann stared challengingly at their battle-weary faces, as if he were expecting one of them to deny the truth of his bald statement.

'Of course you're right, Martin,' Himmler said and wet his dry lips delicately with his mineral water. 'The coming battle here is vital for the Reich, but don't you think you are putting the matter into a too dramatic a light? I mean if you consider—'

'No,' Bormann butted in harshly and von Dodenburg could see that the Golden Pheasant hardly disguised his contempt for the leader of the SS. 'I am not being too dramatic, Heinrich. Let there be no mistake about it. This is a battle for the survival of the Reich. Time is running out. If we don't succeed in crushing the Bolsheviks this summer, we certainly will not be able to do it in the winter. All of us know what happened last winter, don't we?' A few of the assembled officers nodded their heads thoughtfully; Stalingrad and the tremendous debacle there was always at the backs of their minds.

Bormann flashed a hard look around the young faces of the Wotan officers. 'Believe me the Führer is well aware of the great suffering you and your men have undergone. But he knows too that he must demand and receive even greater sacrifices from you in the coming battle. If you were to be at his side like I am, twenty hours a day and saw how he worried about you and Germany, you would know that your sacrifices do not go unnoticed. The loss of one single humble German grenadier cuts the Führer to the heart. Yet he has hardened himself to losses, as he must. You, too, must be harder – as hard as Krupp steel, as they used to say when I was a boy in Mecklenburg. You must ask and get the most brutal sacrifices out of your men in the coming battle. After all the fate of the Third Reich is in your hands.'

He paused, sniffed and looking down at his empty bowl, as if he had already dismissed the 'fate of the Third Reich' from his cold logical mind, he said pleasantly: 'I think I'll have another half litre of that good pea soup, if I may – and half a sausage, if you can spare it, Colonel – er—'

'Geier,' the Vulture snapped, flushing.

'Yes Colonel Geier. Could you arrange it?'

'Metzger,' thundered the Vulture. 'See the Reichsleiter has some more soup. We don't want him to leave the front thinking that we soldiers starve our visitors from the rear echelon, where, as everyone knows, food is in short supply.' The insult was obvious, but the fat Golden Pheasant did not seem to notice it.

'Thank you,' he said pleasantly.

'Don't put yer thumb in that soup, mate,' the tough-looking ex-legionnaire said to the soldier waiter as he passed over the bowl of pea-soup intended for Reichsleiter Bormann. 'It might fall off.'

'Eh!' the other man said surprised.

'Yeah, I just spat in it to season it and I don't think I've been properly cured from the last dose.'

Schulze tossed half a sausage in Bormann's soup. It slopped over the side of the tin bowl. The waiter wiped it off with his sleeve.

'Get on with it,' he growled at the man. 'This comedian here is just having you on. Now trot off, before you get the toe of my boot up your arse.'

Schulze waited until he was out of earshot. 'All right, you asparagus-Tarzan you, what's your plan? And don't try to shit me, or you'll get a taste of the Reeperbahn equalizer.' His hand fell to his pocket.

But the ex-legionnaire was quicker. His hand flashed to his trouser pocket. Before Schulze had even managed to locate his brass knuckles, a wicked, thin-bladed knife appeared in the other man's hand.

'First thing you learn in the Legion, sergeant. In the

compagnie de passage,[2] the old hands like the brown cake. If you don't want to become a warm brother for the rest of your time in the Legion, you learn how to be quick with a knife. Slash-slash to the back of their fat queer arses and they don't bother you again.' He grinned lazily. 'After all, by doing that you've spoiled their good looks, haven't you?' His grin was infectious. Schulze joined him and the ex-legionnaire slipped away the knife as quickly as it had appeared.

'I suppose you're right,' Schulze said. 'Come on, let's take the weight off our feet. I think even that fat little bastard of a Golden Pheasant has finished feeding his face by now.'

In silence they walked to the shade of one of the nearby trees and sat down, their backs against it, watching the men drinking the beer the Reichsführer SS had brought for them in the Storch.

'One bottle between two men,' Schulze snorted. 'That's what I call generous. But then a sniff at the barmaid's apron would send half them greenbeaks over there roaring drunk.'

'I've got half a crate,' the other man said calmly. 'I snitched it while you were cutting up the sausages.'

'Did you just!' Schulze exclaimed in admiration. 'You're a smart lad – too smart to be in this mob.'

'I know and I don't intend to be in it much longer.' The ex-legionnaire pulled out a little shag pipe and the strangest looking tobacco pouch Schulze had ever seen.

'What the hell's that?'

'A Kabyle woman's tit,' he answered, busily stuffing tobacco into his pipe. 'I cut it off and cured it myself in thirty-four. She was a young un – you can tell that by the nipple there and the quality of the skin – never a wrinkle.'

'Put the sodding thing away, will you,' Schulze said in disgust. 'What the hell will some people think of next!'

2. The Legion's training company.

'Caporal Grimaldi had one made out of a Chink's testicles,' the other man said conversationally. 'They were so big you could stow a kilo of baccy in them.' But he put the pouch away and said: 'There are a lot of ways of doing it, you know Sergeant. I wouldn't go as far as infecting an eye with gonorrhea – you can lose it like that – but a bit of tartar from your teeth, rubbed into a wound can cause abscesses. Or perhaps a couple of drops of castor oil in your eye, bandage it up overnight and next morning you've got yourself the start of a nice juicy case of conjunctivitis. Then there's the trick of putting a cork upright in your boot and jumping down with it there from – say – two metres. That's a sure way of dislocating your ankle.'

'All right, laddie, you don't need to draw me no more pictures – I get you. But what does it all add up to? You're still in the Army and when the bone-menders have seen you off, you're back where you started – in SS Assault Battalion Wotan. And you know what that means?'

The legionnaire's calm look vanished. 'Yeah,' he said thickly, the quick chop in double time.'

'Right in one. This is the third time this flaming Battalion has done a stint in Popovland and it's going to be no different from any other, believe you me.' He pointed to the bronzed youths drinking their beer at the trestle tables. 'Most of them greenbeaks over there will be looking at the potatoes from below before this month's out.'

'And you don't intend to be among them, Sarge?'

'No, you ain't shitting, soldier. Mrs Schulze's little boy has had a noseful, right up to here.'

'And how are you gonna pull it off?' the other man asked.

'Never you mind just yet. But I am. The question is, you asparagus Tarzan, can I count on you when the time comes? I need somebody like you who knows the world—'

Before the ex-legionnaire could answer, Metzger was bellowing angrily at them. 'Come on Schulze, what the hell do you think this is – a Jew school or something? The Reichsführer is going and we've got to form up. Come on – get the lead out of your shitty arses, will you?'

The Storch's engine roared. In front of it on the parched yellow steppe, what was left of SS Assault Battalion Wotan stood rigidly to attention beneath the burning white sun. Standing to von Dodenburg's right, the new Colonel Geier had his hand touched to his cap in salute, the sweat pouring off his burned face.

At the door the two important visitors paused. Reichsführer Himmler took a last look at the hard-faced young men who were staring at some far vista. Even above the roar of the plane's engine, he could hear the rumble of the heavies as they began to pound the Soviet position, prior to the great tank attack. Tears of emotion came to his dark eyes. Swiftly he took off his clouded pince-nez that made him look like some provincial schoolmaster and rubbed them clear.

'Comrades,' he said thickly, 'I your Reichsführer, salute you.' He clicked his spindly legs together in the position of attention and flung out his hand in the German greeting. 'Heil Hitler.' Just behind von Dodenburg Schulze strained himself to launch one of his farts as an expression of his contempt for the base stallions who could send so many men to a violent death with so little thought.

But the Golden Pheasant Bormann, standing next to the Reichsführer, beat him to it. He belched loudly, grabbed Himmler by the arm and said carelessly, 'Oh for God's sake, Heinrich, come on. There's fried chicken at the Führer's Headquarters tonight. And if we don't get there soon, that greedy bastard Hoffmann will have eaten it all up.'[3]

3. Presumably this is a reference to 'Professor' Hoffmann, Hitler's fat personal photographer, who was Bormann's deadly enemy (transl.)

THREE: CLASH AT KURSK

'The battle you will join in forty-eight hours' time will be the greatest tank battle in all history, and when you have fought it, those of you who survive will count it as the most significant event in your whole lives.' – *Heinrich Himmler to the officers of Wotan. July 9th, 1943.*

ONE

As the great ball of the crimson sun slid over the horizon, the Russian Major-General braced himself against the lone tree on the hill overlooking the battlefield and focused his glasses on the Fritzes' line.

The debris of war came into view: broken ammo boxes, abandoned jerricans, rusting wire, shattered Russian and German tanks already beginning to sparkle in the sun's first threatening rays. Beyond were the Fritzes' laagers, huge boxes of silent Tigers and Panthers, their great hooded guns hanging low. But in the heavy silence that hung over the battlefield, the Russian General fancied he could hear a faint hammering from the German camp and the clatter of metal against metal. Swiftly he adjusted his glasses. As he had suspected men were hurrying everywhere, getting the tanks ready for the day's great battle.

'The Fritzes are early risers, Comrade General Rotmistrov,' he muttered to his companion, the commander of the Fifth Guards Tank Army.

Rotmistrov, the Red Army's greatest tank expert, looked down at the little Ukrainian politico. 'They are a great people, the Germans, Comrade Khruschev,' he said, carefully concealing his dislike of the other man. 'They work hard and they fight hard.'

'True. Comrade Lenin thought them a great people. For many years he believed that they would start the world revolution. He was mistaken, wasn't he?' Khruschev lowered his glasses and smiled, revealing his misshapen yellow teeth. But there was no corresponding warmth in his eyes. He dug his thumb into his barrel chest. 'But in this I, Nikita Khruschev, will not be wrong, Comrade General. Today, down there on that plain, we Russians, will fight and beat the Fritzes – and we shall beat them so soundly that they will never rise again. Today, Comrade General Rotmistrov, we shall win the war!'

'Rotmistrov,' Schwarz had asked the night before at the briefing, 'is that a Jewish name?'

'I do not know, my dear Schwarz,' the Vulture had answered. 'And I really don't care if his mother were a cross-eyed whore from the Reeperbahn and his father the legendary Polack Yid from Lvov. All that concerns me – and you – is that he is a highly competent Popov tank commander who gave us a bad time at Stalingrad and who will oppose us to-morrow with fifteen hundred tanks!'

That had made the assembled officers start and the Vulture had laughed coldly. 'Yes, I thought that would startle you gentlemen, especially as Colonel-General Hoth can only muster eight hundred tanks and SP to oppose them. In short we will be outnumbered by two to one.'

'But we are the SS, sir,' Schwarz had protested hotly.

For a moment the Vulture had said nothing; then he had tugged at the end of his monstrous beak of a nose and rasped, 'Yes, my dear young Schwarz, we are the SS as you rightly say. Let us hope our Popov friends on the other side of that rise realize that, eh?' But now as the laager broke up with a yelping of locked tracks, the hiss of hydraulics and the thick throaty roar of diesels bursting into life, von Dodenburg could not help feeling a tremendous sense of power, despite the fact that they were so grievously outnumbered. As the tanks fanned out, the first rays of the sun turning their glacis plates blood-red, the sight of so many German tanks deploying for the drive which would take them this day south-east of Kursk, he was overcome by the sense of immense supre-

144

macy. Surely nothing would be able to stop their tremendous drive – even if the Popovs outnumbered them ten to one? Here was the elite of Germany's armour, manned by the best soldiers in the world, each a convinced believer in the holy creed of National Socialism, Europe's only hope against the evil of Communism.

As the Wotan formed up with the Vulture's command Tiger in the centre and started to rumble forward at ten kilometres an hour, the drivers squinting against the sun, the steppe remained empty and uncannily quiet. At von Dodenburg's side in the turret, Schulze tensed, waiting for the first frightening flash on the horizon. But to the young officer, he and the rest of the crew seemed possessed of an animal patience. How else could they stand the terrible wait before the first brazen metal started ripping into them, tearing out tendons, muscles, nerves?

Down below, the new driver whom Schulze had picked from the 8th Division reinforcements revved the engine suddenly. Von Dodenburg jumped nervously. For a moment he was angry with the man.

'Hartmann,' he snapped into the throat mike, but changed his mind and switched off the intercom. He'd probably only been cleaning out a dirty plug or something. Von Dodenburg looked down at his watch again. The minutes were crawling. He licked his dry lips for the umpteenth time.

Here and there some of the younger tank commanders were already buttoning up for the action which must come. But still the horizon remained empty and the sun slanting in at an awkward angle made it difficult for the Germans to see if the Popovs had concealed positions waiting for them. Nothing stirred.

Suddenly a flare hissed into the still morning sky. For what seemed a very long time it hung there, sending out showers of silver sparks into the light blue, before it died and descended to the steppe like a falling angel. But what happened next was in no way angelic. The horizon shook abruptly. There was a sound like a great piece of canvas being ripped apart. Red lights rippled all along the horizon to their right flank. White burning blobs flew towards them, increasing in speed at every moment.

'Anti-tank fire,' the Vulture screamed over the radio. 'Deploy—'

His words were drowned by the great clang of metal against metal. A Mark IV close to von Dodenburg's Tiger reared up on its rear sprockets like a bucking bronco and came to a sudden halt. Solid shot was flying everywhere. Suddenly the air was full of the acrid stink of cordite, scorched metal and burned human-flesh. Von Dodenburg snapped into action.

'Gunner – traverse right . . . Up a hundred . . . Popov 57 mm!'

Hurriedly Schulze swung the great hooded 88 round on the Soviet anti-tank gun, his big fingers working the elevating mechanism almost lovingly. 'On,' he rapped.

'Fire!'

The air in front of the Tiger flashed a bright yellow. The turret rocked like a shaken toy. Blast flew into the turret and the spent shell case rattled to the floor. Von Dodenburg shoved in the next round. Hurriedly he peered through his periscope.

'Short, Schulze,' he yelled.

'Shit!' Schulze cursed.

'Up fifty!'

Schulze's fingers worked the wheel crazily. The next instant he pulled the firing lever. The turret heaved again. Von Dodenburg flung himself on the periscope. His circle of vision was thick with smoke. Abruptly it cleared. Where the Popov 57 mm had been, there was a gaping glowing hole, littered with bits and pieces which had been men a moment before.

'We've got the bastard,' he yelled exuberently. Got him!'

'Christ, sir – *look out*!' Hartmann's voice cut into their cries of triumph urgently. 'There's three of the Ivan bastards at eleven o'clock!'

Schulze reacted first. As the one-armed commander of the Third Company's Tiger blazed and skidded to a sudden halt, he fired. The first Russian anti-tank gun disappeared in a vicious red ball of flame. Immediately the remaining two, cunningly concealed in a slight hollow only three hundred metres away, swung their long barrels onto von Dodenburg's tank. A whooshing rush. That well-remembered frightening whiplash. And the first solid shot hushed by them like a bat out of hell.

'Hartmann,' von Dodenburg shouted frantically into the throat mike. 'Find me a bit of ground. I want to tackle the bastards hull down!'

'Sir!' The ex-legionnaire was a good soldier, there was no denying that. He charged straight into the thick white smoke pouring from Barsch's crippled Tiger. It shielded them a little from the Russians. When it seemed they would crash into the Third Company tank, he swerved swiftly to the right. Immediately he ran up the Tiger's forward gears, bringing her up to top speed while her whole flank was exposed to the Soviet guns. Before the Popovs could range, the Tiger had buried her nose into a slight depression and von Dodenburg was almost flung out of his metal seat with the impact.

'First class, Hartmann!' he bellowed.

'Don't bother about the medal, sir,' the driver replied coolly, not even breathing hard. 'I'll just take an immediate transfer to the paymaster branch.'

Von Dodenburg laughed. 'Schulze engage!' he yelled the

next moment as the enfuriated Russians started pounding the earth in front of their glacis plate with solid shot.

Blinded as he was by earth and flying pebbles, Schulze took careful aim. The long gun erupted. The Tiger reared like a live thing. A high explosive shell crashed into the steppe fifty metres in front of the first Russian gun.

'Short, Schulze,' von Dodenburg cried angrily. 'For Chris-sake man, get your finger out!'

'But sir—'

Schulze's protest was cut short by the chatter of the driver's machine gun below. A vicious burst of white tracer zig-zagged flatly across the scorched steppe and ripped into the fleeing crew of the first Soviet anti-tank gun. The shot had been close enough for them. They were attempting to flee. In vain. Hartmann cut down the first three with his burst, waited till the fourth man feigning death among his dying comrades, risked making a break for it and ripped his body apart neatly before he had gone five metres.

'Will they never learn,' he shouted over the crackling intercom, full now of the static of battle. 'If he'd just have stayed where he was, he might have lived to tell the story to his grandkids.'

'Grandkids,' Schulze snorted, obviously angry with von Dodenburg for his criticism. 'Who in Christ's name would want grandkids – for this!'

'Knock it off, Schulze,' von Dodenburg ordered. 'Plaster that other gun with everything you've got – it's stopping the whole company!'

To their right another Mark IV brewed up menacingly. The tank commander dropped from the cupola, his coverall a mass of angry flames. He rolled himself over to put out the flames. Screaming wildly, he rose to his feet again and ran blindly across the steppe, the flames mounting higher and higher until he crashed into one of their own tanks. The driver did not see him. The man disappeared beneath the Tiger's great tracks. When they reappeared they were covered with a sticky red pulp.

Schulze pulled the firing lever. High explosive burst over the heads of the second Russian crew. Shrapnel pattered onto the shield of the anti-tank gun. A tyre burst and the 57 mm sank to one side. The crew panicked. They began to run. But Hartmann was waiting for them. Again his 7.62 mm spoke. Eight hundred slugs a minute hissed through the air. The Popovs were cut down screaming.

'Excellent, von Dodenburg,' a voice rasped suddenly over the radio. 'But get on the stick again. You're bogging down.' It was the Vulture.

Hastily von Dodenburg pressed the button. 'Yes, sir, will do. Advance on the present bearing?'

'Yes,' the Vulture's voice was as calm as it had ever been on any training exercise in Westphalia. 'I've been observing the Popov fire. It was good to begin with. It's getting worse. They're obviously losing their nerve. The closer we get to that ridge where their anti-tank guns are, the more chance we have. They won't be able to depress the sodding guns enough to hit us. Are you with me?'

'Yessir.'

'Good – and good hunting, von Dodenburg.'

'Thank you, sir.'

As the First Company started to advance again in extended order, von Dodenburg's mouth fell open. The smoke of war cleared for a moment. Immediately the Popov anti-tank guns on the ridge began firing again. But it wasn't the guns; it was what lay beyond them. From one side of the horizon to the other, there was nothing but solidly massed Soviet tanks – hundreds, no thousands of them! Next to him in the yellow, smoke-filled turret, Schulze breathed in an awed voice:

149

'Great crap on the Christmas Tree, do you see that, sir?'

Von Dodenburg could not answer. He was afraid: more afraid than he had ever been in his life before. Slowly, inexorably, the two great masses of machines began to close in on each other.

The Führer's knuckles whitened – a sign of inner tension – as the grey-clad 'field mattresses' [1] added more and more newly identified Soviet formations to the great table map of the Eastern front. They were not just battalions, or regiments, but whole divisions, corps, armies! The backs of the girls' thick uniforms were stained black with sweat, as they hurried to the table from the telephones, to place yet another counter on it. Adolf Hitler turned to a pale-faced Jodl, his face aghast.

'My God, Jodl, where are the Bolsheviks getting the men from?' Without waiting for an answer, he said hoarsely, 'Have you checked with Gehlen that these identifications are correct?'

Major Buechs, Jodl's highly intelligent aide, who had played such a decisive role in planning the great invasion of the West in 1940, butted in.

'I think we can rely on General Gehlen, my Führer. His identifications are realistic.'

Hitler turned on him angrily, glad to have found a victim, a chance to vent his rage.

'Good, Buechs, but does Gehlen know the actual strength of these Bolshevik formations? Are we sure that when we talk of a Soviet regiment, it is not really of battalion strength?'

'Naturally the Russians have reduced the strength of their formations, my Führer, just as we have. But when Gehlen speaks of a regiment, he means a regiment.'

1. German Army slang for the female army auxiliaries (transl.)

Adolf Hitler's sickly face flushed a hectic red. Jodl looking at him, told himself that the man wouldn't last a year, in spite of all the dope that his Doctor Morrell – charlatan that he was – was pumping into him.

'Thank you, Beuchs, you may dismiss,' Hitler said stiffly.

Buechs, his face set angrily, clicked his heels and marched out as if he were on parade. Jodl laughed to himself. He had stood the Führer's moods for four years; it would take more than that to rile him.

Urgently Hitler grabbed his arm. 'Blondi – come,' he commanded hoarsely. The big Alsatian bitch, her tongue hanging out in the heat, rose lazily from the floor and followed them outside. The leaden oppressive heat struck them in the face like a clammy fist. In the firs the SS bodyguard shook themselves awake and gripped their weapons more firmly in their sweaty fists. As the two men began to stroll through the white Ukrainian dust, their heads bent deep in conversation, they followed them like evil black shadows.

'Jodl, I've never liked the Citadel idea. You and your comrades of the Greater German General Staff talked me into it. Now look what kind of a mess you've got me into.'

'Yes, my Führer,' Jodl said dutifully. 'Victory has many fathers,' he told himself cynically, 'defeat, however—' He left the thought unfinished; the Führer was speaking again.

'But where in heaven's name, have the Bolsheviks got such strength from? We knew they outnumbered us. But fifteen hundred tanks and ever new vehicles pouring onto the battlefield! I ask you, it is hardly believable. Jodl, what do you say?'

But Jodl was not prepared to comfort him as he had always done at such moments in the past. The Führer would finally have to face up to reality. National Socialist Germany was losing the war.

Hitler's restless brain moved more quickly than that of his chief aide.

'Good,' he said suddenly, stopping and gripping Jodl by the arm. 'If we cannot put the same kind of armour into the field that the Soviets can, we must compensate some other way.' He smiled suddenly, the smile of a crazy man. 'Why didn't I think of it before?'

'Think of what, my Führer?' Jodl asked dutifully, his body suddenly tense to face what might soon come. He knew only too well what the Führer's hunches were like.

'Rudel – Rudel, of course!' Hitler said eagerly. 'Colonel Rudel of the Luftwaffe. Whatever else one might say of Goering's Luftwaffe, there is no denying Rudel's ability and bravery. How many times has he been wounded since the beginning of hostilities?'

'Nine times, my Führer,' Jodl answered promptly, wondering again why he, as Chief-of-Staff, should be expected to remember such trivia. Yet at the same time he knew that if he didn't, he wouldn't last twenty-four hours in Hitler's entourage. 'Twice severely.'

'That just shows,' Hitler said enthusiastically. 'A man like that, still flying and fighting after so many wounds.' He smashed his right fist into the palm of his left hand. 'A man like that is worth a whole Soviet corps!' All right, Jodl, inform Luftwaffe headquarters that I want Colonel Rudel's five squadrons of tank hunters to join the battle immediately – do you understand, immediately?' But before Jodl could muster the expected enthusiasm, Buechs came running out of the conference room, his face wild with shock.

'My Führer,' he called. 'My Führer!'

'What is it, Buechs?' Hitler snapped.

The Major thrust the flimsy message into Hitler's hand. 'Just arrived from Field Marshal Rommel, my Führer – most immediate,' he gasped.

Hitler took it out of his hand, his face still flushed with the enthusiasm of his sudden decision. Awkwardly he fumbled for the gold-rimmed spectacles in which Hoffmann was never allowed to photograph him. Finally he focused them on the message. A long animal groan rose from deep within him. A muscle in the side of his face began to tick dangerously,

'What is it, my Führer?' Jodl asked in alarm, putting out his hands as if he might have to support his leader.

Wordlessly Hitler handed the top secret message to him. It was simple and to the point, but Jodl knew Rommel's handful of words meant the end of the Thousand Year Reich.

'ALLIES LANDED SICILY THIS MORNING.

ROMMEL.'

TWO

It was furnace-hot now. The glare cut the eye like a knife. Above the waiting panzers the sky was smoke-coloured and menacing. Through it the sun glittered like a copper coin. But despite the murderous heat, they were ready, the identification panel spread out across the fronts of their tanks, the huge arrows draped over the burned charred grass pointing in the direction of the Soviet lines. The tank hunters could come now.

'There they are!' Schulze yelled suddenly and pointed up to the west.

'Here they come!' the men of Wotan took up the cry everywhere, clambering up on the decks of the stalled Tigers

153

and Mark IVs to get a better view, heedless of the fact that there were still Popov snipers about.

Like black hawks they came roaring in from the sun. A whole squadron of Stuka tank busters. Now they hovered over the battlefield, poised to fall on their prey. Suddenly the leader moved his bent-hawk wings. Once, twice, three times. it was the signal.

The first flight peeled off. The first black shape came roaring down, its sirens screaming hideously. Immediately the Popov flak beyond the rise snapped into action. Puff-balls of cotton-white erupted all around the Stuka, but Colonel Rudel, the Luftwaffe's ace, pressed home his attack. Just when he seemed about to plunge into the churned, battle-littered earth at 400 mph, he levelled out. A myriad of black eggs fell from the Stuka's white-painted belly. The earth around the first Popov armoured position vomited up-wards in ugly black clouds.

On the panzers the troopers yelled with joy. As Rudel soared high into the sky, vicious red and yellow flames split the black pall. T-34 after T-34 was hit. White and green tracer ammunition zig-zagged crazily in all directions.

'Go on, give it to the Bolshevik bastards!' they cried in frenzied excitement as the next Stuka hurtled down.

The air became a thick choking fog of yellow steppe dust and dense oily smoke. The whole battlefield was one mon-strous din through which the SS men could faintly hear the tortured cries of wounded and dying Russians. And then, as suddenly as it had started, the attack stopped. The flak dwindled to isolated bangs. The noise of Stukas grew fainter and fainter as they flew back the way they had come, leaving behind a wrecked Russian first line.

But Rudel's tank busters were not finished yet. The Stukas had hardly vanished when there was the drone of fresh planes from the west. Almost instantly two squadrons of Henschel 129 took shape on the horizon. Immediately all eyes flashed in that direction. Von Dodenburg's dirty face lit up.

'There are more of them. Now we'll show the Popovs!'

'They're not tanks though,' Schulze said dourly, as the roar grew louder. 'They're still not tanks.'

'Oh go on, you ray of sunshine,' von Dodenburg said, shielding his eyes against the glare and studying the cannon-bearing tank busters – eighteen of them in all, already breaking up into their attack formation.

One flight turned slightly to the east, another swung west while a third kept to the centre so that they were spread out like the three prongs of an enormous hay fork. The Soviet flak swung into action. A Henschel staggered visibly in the sky. Thick white smoke started to pour from its starboard engine. The pilot tried to hold it, but failed. Carefully he began to lose height, obviously nursing his crippled plane down for an emergency landing on the steppe. With anxious eyes the men of Wotan began to follow him down, their sweating fists clenched tensely. Suddenly the Henschel burst into a gigantic ball of flame. It shattered into a million pieces, snuffed out like a candle. The rest of the formation flew on steadily.

Now they were over the Soviet positions. The leader of the first flight flapped his wings. In the same instant he threw his plane into a dive. At three hundred miles an hour they came roaring down, their cannon firing.

All hell broke loose in the Soviet lines. The first wave swept in at one hundred and fifty metres, their under-carriages down acting as a brake. The 20 mm shells came streaming from their wings. T-34 after T-34 brewed up suddenly. The watchers on the ground could see panic-stricken Russian tankers abandoning their vehicles even before they were hit. Time and time again the Henschels came in at ground level, twisting and weaving crazily to avoid the Popov flak before pulling up in a back-breaking climb in order to do it again.

On the waiting Tigers, the crews yelled themselves hoarse, waving their arms frantically, as the Henschels roared in low over their heads, the white blobs of their pilots' heads clearly visible.

But this time the Luftwaffe was not going to have it all their own way. The Soviets had been alarmed. From the east swarms of Yak fighters roared into the battle. The sky was criss-crossed from horizon to horizon by scores of white vapour trails, as the planes weaved back and forth in single combat. But the Henschels were no match for the swifter, more nimble Yaks. One after one they were shot from the skies.

One crippled Henschel, thick white smoke pouring from its riddled engine, came screaming into their laager. It hit the ground, sprang up a good thirty metres, hit the steppe again and somersaulted to a stop. Another crashed between two trees, its wings snapping off like twigs. Its pilot stepped out with a shaky grin on his deathly pale face and asked for a schnapps; then he fainted.

But he was one of the lucky ones. The Yaks knocked the slower-moving Henschels out of the sky everywhere, screaming in low over the German tanks, executing flashy barrel rolls to demonstrate their victory to the impotent tankers. And then it was all over and what was left of the Henschels were fleeing to the west, leaving the sky in the hands of the Russians.

Schulze spat drily into the dust and watched as the smoke began to clear over the Soviet positions. When it did, it was clear that the Popovs had been hurt. Scores of tanks were crippled and burning all over the scorched Steppe. But behind them hundreds more waited, black squat impassive shapes, their cannon now swinging round to face the Germans again.

'Hell,' he commented sourly. 'I've closed my eyes twice, but the sods won't go away, Hartmann.'

The ex-legionnaire's usual lazy, cynical smile was absent. 'Well, sarge, if *they* won't go away—' he stopped abruptly and looked Schulze directly in the face.

'I read you, Hartmann,' Schulze said slowly. 'You don't need to send me no telegram. If they won't go away, we must, eh?'

Before Hartmann could answer, the officers began blowing their whistles. Tanks' motors burst into noisy life. Von Dodenburg ran back from the Vulture's command Tiger, holding on to his pistol holster.

'Mount up,' he cried. 'Mount up. We're going to attack before the Ivans recover again.'

The bombardment started with the roar of an infuriated beast. Countless flashes of violent fire cut the plain behind them. A deafening thunder. The next instant the whole weight of the corps artillery hit the Soviet first line of attack. The earth shuddered. Even behind the thick armour of their Tiger they could feel the blast. Automatically they opened their mouths to prevent their ear drums being burst.

'Enemy tanks – two o'clock,' an unknown voice crackled over the radio. 'Thousands of the bastards!'

Von Dodenburg flung a quick glance around the gloomy turret. The red control light showed a black FA sign. All guns were cleared. He looked at Schulze crouched over his eyepiece. They were ready for action. He threw a quick glance through the look-out slit. The smoking landscape in front of him was jammed with Soviet tanks and SPs. Tank after tank crawling forward to them.

Over the radio the Vulture's voice rasped, almost cheerfully for once. 'Now, gentlemen, I think it is time that we exercised our calling. Roll them!'

Hartmaan put the sixty-ton monster in gear. To their left and right the line of Wotan's tanks began to move out to meet the enemy. There was the typewriter chatter of a Soviet machine gun. The golden-white tracer scudded off their cupola like crazy gold balls.

'Don't fire, Schulze,' von Dodenburg ordered quickly. 'They're only ranging in.'

'I wasn't going to, sir,' Schulze said with unusual quietness. He looked like a man who was fighting some inner battle. But at that moment von Dodenburg had not time enough to concern himself with the problem. His blood-shot eyes were searching their immediate front, while he counted the number of Popov T-34s facing Wotan's forty odd tanks. When he had reached one hundred and fifty, he gave up in despair.

Schwarz's Second began the action. They were slightly to the right and in advance of the rest of the Battalion. As usual, Schwarz was eager for glory and battle. He got both. Suddenly his dozen mixed Tigers and Mark IVs picked up speed and went straight for an enormous concentration of T-34s.

'For Chrissake, Schwarz,' von Dodenburg began, but the words died on his lips.

The strange somnambulist advance of the Russians stopped abruptly. Frantically the Soviet gunners swung their 76s round to concentrate on the Germans. Everywhere the commanders were up in their turrets, waving their flags like crazy boy scouts.

Schwarz's gunners did not miss the excellent target. Red tracer hissed across the gap between the two groups. Soviet tank commanders went down everywhere. Hastily turret flaps closed and the Soviet gunners pulled their firing levers.

Pillars of white smoke flew up on all sides, as the Soviets fired wildly into the daring little handful of Germans. Over the radio, Schwarz's voice crackled exuberently.

'We've got them rattled, men. Come on now. Let's show them what SS Assault Battalion Wotan is made of!'

The 88s and 75s burst into life. Solid shot tore flatly through the burning air. The next instant the shells were crashing into the Soviet armour with a sound like a smith beating an anvil. Suddenly the radio was full of orders and cries of rage or triumph. 'T-34 firing now . . . by that scrub . . . hit him low. *Fire*. . . . Christ on a crutch, you missed! . . . Up a hundred . . . *up a hundred*! I said . . . That's it . . . fire again!' Almost at once the battle developed into a confused dogfight. Raw jabs of flame pierced the oily smoke, followed instants later by the great crump of another tank brewing up.

Schwarz was right in among the Russians now. T-34s were flaming everywhere. But his own tanks were suffering serious casualties. As the rest of the Battalion fringed the skirmish, rolling inexorably to the mass of the Russian attack, they could see how vehicle after vehicle was being hit.

'My Christ, look at that!' Schulze yelled suddenly and dug von Dodenburg in the ribs painfully.

The cheerful blond giant who had carried the grenades on the first day of the attack was swaying on the engine covers of a burning Tiger, trying to haul out someone inside. At first von Dodenburg thought he was kneeling. Then he saw his mistake. The giant had balanced himself on the two bloody stumps of what had been his legs. Behind him the wooden boxes containing the 7.62 machine gun ammo were beginning to burn.

'Jump,' von Dodenburg yelled into the throat mike purposelessly. 'For God's sake, jump, man!'

But the blond giant could not hear. Next instant the

nearest wooden box erupted and the giant disappeared in a blinding white blaze.

Now Schwarz was all alone. His company had vanished, swamped by the sheer weight of the T-34s. On all sides the Russians concentrated their fire on his lone Tiger. Still he did not make smoke and try to retreat. A 76 mm caught him in the flank. The Tiger rocked as if on a rough sea; ugly red sparks flew from the rear sprocket. For a moment it was obscured in smoke. Von Dodenburg, his hands damp with sweat, peered through his periscope helplessly. But when the smoke cleared, the Tiger was still moving forward, though at a reduced speed.

'Lieutenant Schwarz, I order you to break off the action,' the Vulture's voice. 'Do you hear, Schwarz. Break it off *now*!'

The only answer was a crazy cackle over the radio, distorted even more by the static as half a dozen T-34s concentrated their fire on the Tiger. The huge tank heeled back and forth. Great gleaming metal scars appeared suddenly all along its right side. A thin white stream of smoke began to escape from the engine cowling. Still the metal monster rolled on, its great gun swinging from left to right, as the gunner attempted to fend off the final attack.

The Soviet fire intensified angrily. Another T-34 flamed and the crew scrambled madly out of the escape hatches to be mown down without mercy. Then a lucky Soviet shot snapped a track pin on the left track. It flopped out behind the Tiger like a broken limb. The tank gave a great lurch and came to a sudden stop. Schwarz, crazy as he was, reacted at once. He made smoke.

'For God's sake, run for it, Schwarz!' the Vulture yelled over the radio as the thick white fumes enveloped the dying Tiger. Schwarz did so. But he was cunning enough to let his crew go first. In a panic-stricken bunch they appeared suddenly out of the white fog to be mown down by the concentrated fire of a dozen Soviet machine guns.

'Arse up, Heil Stalin!' Schulze cursed, his voice full of helpless bitterness. 'Why the hell did they bunch like that—'

He broke off suddenly. Schwarz had appeared from the smoke. He was on his stomach, a Schmeisser in one hand, the other thick with blood streaming from a shattered shoulder. Cautiously he glanced left and right and began to crawl for the cover of a knocked-out T-34, its dead crew sprawled out carelessly around it. Five metres – ten. Schwarz seemed to be in luck. While Wotan rolled ever closer to the mass of the Soviet tanks, von Dodenburg could not drag his eyes off the little officer squirming his way through the dust to safety. It seemed to him at that moment that if Schwarz made it, they would too.

Suddenly the Soviets discovered him. Angry tracer sliced the air low. Schwarz stumbled to his feet, his blood dripping into the dust. Awkwardly he began to stagger for cover, lead stitching a fiery trail at his feet.

'Come on, come on,' von Dodenburg heard himself crying and felt the sweat pour from his body. 'For Chrissake, Schwarz, do it!'

But a rapid burst caught Schwarz in the back.

'*Sch-warz!*' von Dodenburg bawled. Schwarz's knees buckled. His arms dangled as his body lost its ability to stay upright. The Schmeisser clattered out of his nerveless fingers. Slowly Schwarz sank to the ground, and as the first of Wotan's 88s cracked into action, von Dodenburg knew that they could not win now.

THREE

Colonel Jodl gave the details with cold clinical precision, while the Führer, his senior generals and the staff listened in stiff-backed, rigid silence.

'Montgomery has put his Eighth Army ashore here. We've already identified his 12 and 30 Corps – both from the Desert. That cowboy Patton has landed personally with his Seventh Army here.' He smiled coldly, but his clever eyes did not light up. 'No doubt we shall be seeing him do it personally in the next US Army newsreel we capture. That man certainly has an eye for personal publicity.' He tapped the big man of Sicily with his elegantly manicured hand. 'They've got Syracuse already and undoubtedly they will take Gela soon. No doubt our Allies will put up a show of resistance on the Catanian Plain.' He did not attempt to hide his contempt at the expense of the Italians. 'But I'll give Montgomery a week. As slow as he is, he'll be on the Straits of Messina, this time next week.'

'So that's it,' Model said brutally, summing up what all of them were thinking. 'We've lost Sicily.' He fixed his monocle more firmly and glared at Hitler as if he were personally responsible. 'This means the end of Operation Citadel, what?'

Hitler did not notice the look, but he came straight to the point. The new threat seemed to have cleared his mind; he was his old self. 'Thanks to the miserable leadership of the Italians it is as good as certain that Sicily will be lost,' he said. 'Maybe Eisenhower will land tomorrow on the Italian mainland or in the Balkans. When that happens our entire

162

European south flank will be directly threatened. I must prevent that.'

Slowly he walked to the window, clenching and unclenching his fists, as if he were working out the problem within himself, weighing up, first one point and then the other. Outside the black-uniformed guards lurked in the firs, always watchful. Blondi lay sprawled in the dusty shade, her long purple tongue hanging out as she gasped for air. It was terribly hot again despite the earliness of the hour.

Hitler turned suddenly and faced his generals. 'I need divisions for Italy, gentlemen. Since they can't be taken from any other place, they must come from Russia.'

'Kursk?' Model snapped.

'Yes, Model. Kursk. I'll move the First Panzer Division from France to the Peloponnese. But I need more armour down in the south so that I can move quickly wherever the Anglo-Americans strike. I'll have to take most of Hoth's armour, or at least his SS Corps. They're his best.'

'They *were*,' Jodl told himself for he had just seen the latest casualty figures, but naturally he did not say that to the Führer, who snapped:

'Jodl, order the SS Corps to be withdrawn immediately.

'But that means the end of Citadel, as I have already stated,' Model persisted, his face flushing an even deeper red than normal.

Hitler turned on him. 'For the time being, Model.' He clenched his fists and his face hardened, full of the fire which had taken him out of the Viennese slums to be the head of Europe's greatest nation. 'But we shall go back, Model. Believe you me – *we shall go back*!'

Jodl sighed and mentally began making out the withdrawal order for the SS Corps, while the Führer and his generals stared at each other in tense silence.

163

'Attention all commanders . . . attention all commanders,' the Vulture's voice snapped through the static. 'I say again *hold your fire!* Gentlemen, I'd like to wish you luck.' For the first time in four years that he had known him, von Dodenburg sensed a note of emotion in the CO's voice. 'And good shooting!'

'Good shooting,' Schulze snorted as the radio went dead again. 'We'll need more than flaming good shooting to cope with them Ivans sods out there.'

'Hold your wind,' von Dodenburg snapped and concentrated on the Popov tanks coming ever closer.

'Crap said the King and a thousand arseholes bent and took the strain, for in those days the word of the King was law,' Schulze muttered sourly under his breath. But he, too, busied himself with his sight.

There must be at least a hundred Popov tanks rumbling towards them, von Dodenburg told himself grimly, more than the whole Bodyguard could probably muster after yesterday's hellish fighting. Panting suddenly, for no reason that he could analyse, he watched the midday sun catch the serrations on the protective spare tracks that the Popovs had slung over their glacis plates. The T-34s were buttoned down, obviously ready for battle, and von Dodenburg knew that the Popovs, like them, were adjusting their range scales, checking their controls, ready with the next round at the command to fire.

He flung a glance to left and right, checking the Vulture's dispositions. The CO had put his remaining tanks in pretty good positions. He had taken over the remnants of Schwarz's Second and given them the advantage of some shallow hillocks so that they could take up a hull defensive position if necessary. The Third, over to his own right flank, had been given a more mobile role and were hurrying to outflank the Russian attack. For his part, his six remaining Tigers would hold the centre, relying on the strength of their glacis plate armour to withstand any concentrated Russian fire – that was as long as they could keep the Russians at a distance with their own superior 88s.

Their defence was excellent, yet the Soviet force rumbling into the attack was awesome, even after yesterday's tremendous numbers. Even in his wildest dreams, he had never seen so much enemy armour. Suddenly the second-lieutenant, who now commanded the 3rd, broke into his consciousness, his voice distorted by fear.

'Attention all stations . . . attention all stations! I'm going to engage now. Range three hundred metres . . . And wish me luck!' the fearful young voice stopped abruptly.

Von Dodenburg swung his periscope round hurriedly. To his right, the first Mark IV fired – and missed.

'Stupid bastard!' he cursed aloud. 'You should have waited!'

But the Tiger next to the Mark IV scored a hit with his first shot and the radio crackled with hoarse cheers. A T-34 went up in a sudden ball of flame.

'Christ on a crutch – and another!' Schulze yelled over the intercom, as a squat shape was suddenly arrested and a trailer of inky smoke started to rise from it, staining the glittering summer sky. The Popov crew bailed out, to fold instantly, as the machine gun bullets hit them.

The Soviet commander – he had to be a general officer with so many vehicles under his command – reacted at once. Leaving a dozen T-34s to swing round and slug it out, glacis to glacis with the 3rd, he increased the speed of the rest of his formation. They streaked forward at fifty kilometres an hour, bouncing up and down over the steppe on their excellent Christie suspension, firing as they did so. The distance between them and the waiting Wotan narrowed. Five hundred . . . four hundred . . . three hundred and fifty . . . three hundred metres.

'Surely, we've got to open fire –' von Dodenburg began.

The Vulture's voice cut in coldly, the emotional note gone now. It was as if he were giving orders on some peacetime range outside Berlin. 'We're going into the hull down position now, von Dodenburg. Engage them at will . . . Ensure they don't outflank you—' The rest was drowned by the metallic buffeting of two AP shells striking their glacis plate and zooming off again at a forty-five degree angle.

'*Fire!*' von Dodenburg roared.

The 88 erupted with a thick crump. The Tiger shuddered and the breech came racing back to eject the smoking yellow shell-case. To their immediate front, the T-34 which had hit them, came to an abrupt stop. Nothing happened. No one bailed out. There was no flame. Nothing. But the Popov tank neither moved nor fired again.

'Damn fine shot, Schulze!' von Dodenburg yelled exhuberantly. 'Let's have more of the same.' He rammed home another gleaming shell.

Schulze needed no urging. The T-34s were coming in at the six lone Tigers from all sides now. The sweat pouring down his back, staining his shirt back, he pumped shell after shell into the attackers. Von Dodenburg flung a glance at the shell bins. They were emptying fast. The floor was covered with empty shell cases. But they dare not let up. Once they did, the Soviets would come in for the kill. Now their immediate front was littered with burning Soviet tanks, their crews sprawled out in the blackened grass or hanging dead from the turrets. But there seemed no end to them, and they were oblivious to their tremendous losses. The first Tiger bought it, outflanked by a T-34 which had sneaked to the flank under the cover of smoke and hit it in the rear sprocket.

166

'*Close up!*' von Dodenburg screamed over the radio. '*Close up, sod you* . . . Do you want the bastards to get in among us!'

Hurriedly the two Tigers holding the flanks reversed closer to the remaining three. Too late! Three T-34s pounced on the Tiger to the left. 76 mm shells smashed into its side. It heeled as if it had been struck by the great wind. Metal lava erupted from its side. A tongue of flame licked lazily around the engine cowling followed by thick white smoke. But von Dodenburg had no further time for the stricken Tiger. The Russian commander had spotted his chance. Five further T-34s broke away from the main body and roared in after the three which had knocked out the flank Tiger.

'Everybody – everybody!' von Dodenburg yelled frantically. 'Concentrate on those T-34s to the left. *Fire!*'

Schulze, good soldier that he was, reacted first. He pumped three quick shots at the advancing T-34s. One went wild, but the other two hit their targets. Down below Hartmann pressed the trigger of his machine gun. The Popov crews were cut down before they'd gone five metres. But the remaining six came rattling on, heading straight into the flank of von Dodenburg's formation. Another Tiger was hit and disappeared in a spectacular ball of crazy orange flame. The shell must have hit the ammunition bin.

Von Dodenburg was no longer afraid, just angry. He had never been so angry in his whole life before: angry with the Popovs, his inexperienced crews, the war, himself. 'Hartmann,' he yelled over the intercom. 'We will advance!'

'*What!*' the ex-legionnaire roared back.

'You heard me – or have you been eating big beans! We will advance!'

'But Captain—'

'If you don't move this metal bitch in one second, I'll blow your shitty brains out and move it myself! March or croak! All right, you'd better march!' Hartmann 'marched'.

The dispatch rider slewed his dust-covered bike round dramatically and let it drop to the steppe behind the Vulture's Tigers, waiting for the Soviet attack to swamp them. Doubled low, he pelted towards the command vehicle. With the butt of his schmeisser he hammered at the metal while the first Soviet ranging shells whizzed over his head.

'Open up!' he screamed with fear as they came ever closer. 'Open up the crappy lid, won't you!'

Finally his hammering was heard. The Vulture poked his head out. Metzger's followed.

'What's the matter?' the Vulture yelled.

The DR cupped his hands around his mouth against the mounting thunder of the guns. 'Dispatch from division, sir!' he cried, his eyes fixed on the Soviet tanks getting ever closer. 'Here.' He thrust the message into the Vulture's hands.

Hastily the Vulture read through it. 'Good. Give me the message form.'

Swiftly the Vulture scribbled a few words, while the Soviet shells began to creep towards them and the tank gunners started to adjust their range.

'There. See that gets to the General.'

The DR snatched the message. 'Yessir!' he yelled and dropped off the deck. Crouched low, he doubled back to his bike and kicked it back into noisy life. The next instant he was off in a tremendous cloud of dust, as if the whole of the Red Army were after him. The Vulture chuckled, pleased with the message.

'What is it, sir?' Metzger asked anxiously, his eyes flicking continually to the advancing Soviet monsters.

'We shall live to fight another day, Metzger. We have been ordered to withdraw immediately.'

'Thank God for that, sir,' Metzger said with an overwhelming sense of relief.

'Yes, at least I'll still be in the running for those general's stars. Those fat-arsed base stallions won't get all the promotion that comes out of this war. Now, Metzger, get your head out of the way. Let's button up before those Popovs knock it off.'

Swiftly he dropped inside the cupola and picked up the mike.

'Make smoke,' the CO yelled over the radio. 'Make smoke and move out. *Now*!'

The frightened young tank commanders needed no urging. The Popovs were almost upon them now. All along their line the black smoke containers hissed into the air and burst over their turrets with soft plops. Engines sprang into life. Hastily the drivers flung the tanks into reverse. The sixty-ton monsters backed out of the hollow, firing as they went.

The Tiger bounced and came to a sudden stop. Down below Hartmann screamed like a woman.

'Deschner' – he meant the co-driver – 'he's been hit, sir . . . The top of his head has come off!'

For a moment von Dodenburg did not seem to digest the news. His head was ringing like a metal bell and the turret was filled with a strange echoing sound that would not die. Then he saw the thick white smoke which had started to stream up from below. Suddenly the turret was filled with acrid choking fumes.

He shook his head violently and yelled, 'Bale out . . . she's going to blow!'

There was another devastating explosion close by. The stricken Tiger rocked violently. The T-34s were confident now. They had crippled the German; they were coming in for the kill. Von Dodenburg crouched and blinking in the biting smoke, peered inside the driving compartment.

Deschner was sitting upright in his seat still, his hand clasped on the machine gun handle, as if he were just about to fire it. But his head was absent. It lay on the littered deck, the radio earphones still attached, grinning up at him. Sickened, von Dodenburg swung himself up again. There was nothing they could do for Deschner – and Hartmann had already bailed out.

'All right, Schulze,' he yelled, as the first flames started to lick up around his feet. 'Get out of here – quick!'

Heavy smoke was everywhere, obscuring everything, pouring a putrid smother over their own stricken Tiger. Pressing his body close to the turret ring, he rolled over it, out and dropped onto the steppe. On the other side Schulze did the same. The blast buffeted him across the face. Somewhere close by a Russian machine gun chattered. Tracer zipped past him. He struggled to his feet. He felt unutterably weary. All he wanted to do was to lie down on the churned earth, close his eyes and drift into sleep, forgetting the tragedy with had struck his company.

Schulze loomed up out of the smoke, his face black and bleeding from a nasty gash over the right eye. Hartmann followed, his helmet off, struggling with his pistol belt. Finally he got the buckle undone and threw it down with a gesture of contempt.

'What's that for, Hartmann?' von Dodenburg asked shakily.

'I've had enough . . . I'm buggering off,' Hartmann snarled and ducked as another shell exploded close by.

Von Dodenburg wiped the dirt off his face and stared at Hartmann open-mouthed.

'What did you say?' he asked finally.

170

'You heard . . . I'm buggering off. We're all buggering off.'

'But you can't do that! That's desertion in the face of the enemy,' he protested wildly. 'They'll stand you up against a wall for that.'

In his sudden anger, von Dodenburg did not notice the quick wink Hartmann gave Schulze.

'They can have their sodding war, Captain,' Hartmann said, while Schulze moved behind the shocked young officer. 'We've had it! Don't you see?' The ex-legionnaire's eyes bulged from his head with rage. 'Germany's lost the shitting war. The fucking Popovs have beaten us. Now it's everybody for himself. And if you were smart, Captain, you'd do the same.'

Frantically von Dodenburg fumbled for his pistol. 'Hartmann,' he rapped above the noise of the Soviet advance, which was now sweeping towards the Vulture's positions, 'you must be out of your head! This is only one battle. Germany isn't finished by a long chalk. Christ, man, how the devil can you talk such—'

Captain von Dodenburg never finished the sentence. What felt like a brick wall fell on the back of his head. The burning horizon tilted, righted itself, then tilted again. His eyes swung upwards, suddenly sightless. He gasped harshly as his legs splayed out from beneath him and he blacked out . . .

On the hilltop overlooking the battlefield, General Rotmistrov lowered his binoculars and rubbed the circles they had made on his cheeks. Beside him the squat politico looked a moment longer at the retreating Germans before doing the same.

'The Fritzes are running,' he said slowly, almost as if he had to convince himself that what he had just seen was no illusion.

'You said they would, Comrade Khrushchev,' Rotmistrov said.

The Ukrainian grinned. 'I know, but I didn't quite believe myself, then, Comrade General,' he answered.

Rotmistrov smiled in spite of his dislike of the other man. On this great day, he could not be angry with him even though he was always interfering in matters which were the concern of the Stavka [1] alone. 'And now Comrade Khrushchev – what now?'

Khrushchev flung out a pudgy, dirty-nailed hand in the direction of Wotan's fleeing tanks. The survivors had broken through their own smoke-screen and were clattering off to the west at top speed.

'We march, Comrade General – we march to the west,' he exclaimed.

'And our objective?'

'The objective,' the future dictator repeated the question thoughtfully. 'The objective, General Rotmistrov! That is simple. It is Berlin.'

1. The Soviet General Staff.

FOUR: THE YANKS ARE COMING

Amis everywhere! They must breed like shitting rabbits in the United States of shitting America!'

SS Man Schulze to Major von Dodenburg, Sept. 20th, 1943

ONE

The camouflaged Opel Wanderer which had driven him from Aeroporto dell' Uba stopped to let the column of undersized, black-shirted Militia shuffle by, the white dust powdering their shabby boots. They were singing:

> 'Tutto le sere, sotto quel fanal
> presso la caserne . . .
> Con ti Lili Marlene
> con ti Lili Marlene . . .'

But there was no enthusiasm in their liquid Italian voices, just cynicism and war weariness. The big tough para guarding the HQ spat in the dust as they passed, his contempt for their Italian allies unconcealed.

'Sodding macaronis,' he grunted as von Dodenburg got out of the staff car. Then he recognised the major's stars and the death's head badge on the cap, which surmounted von Dodenburg's bandaged head. He snapped to attention. 'Good morning sir,' he bellowed, as if he were on parade.

Carefully Major von Dodenburg touched his hand to his cap. 'Good morning, Corporal. I wonder if you can help me?'

The para clicked to attention again, his rubber-soled jumpboots making a very unsatisfactory sound on the burning hot asphalt.

'Sir!'

'I'm looking for the HQ of SS Assault Battalion Wotan.'

'You mean Battle Group Wotan, sir,' the broken-nosed para corrected him. 'Oh, that's across the square and down

175

that side-street, past the Eyetie knocking shops – oh, excuse me, sir. I mean the Italian brothels, sir.'

Von Dodenburg smiled a little wearily. 'I know what a knocking shop is, Corporal. Thank you.' He touched his hand to his cap again and keeping to the shade he went in the direction indicated by the para.

'Shitty SS,' the corporal muttered behind his back and made an obscene gesture with his middle finger. 'Arrogant bastards – think the sun shines out of their arseholes!'

Slowly, feeling the sweat trickling down the small of his back in the September heat, von Dodenburg made his way towards the Wotan's new headquarters. The paras of Student's Airborne Corps[1] were digging in everywhere. Obviously, von Dodenburg told himself, they were expecting trouble. Even if the Amis didn't drop paratroops on Rome, there was a damn good chance that the Italians would break out of the 'Pact of Steel' and start fighting their former allies. Whatever happened, he thought as he reached the blessed shade of the entrance to Wotan's HQ and showed his pass to the SS sentry, Wotan would be in action soon even if the Amis were still crawling up Italy like a lazy bug on a boot.

Metzger, dressed in summer uniform, clicked to attention when he saw von Dodenburg. 'Major von Dodenburg, sir. Glad to see you again, sir.'

'Thank you, Metzger.' The officer's eye fell on the new decoration on the NCO's burly chest. 'Wound medal in silver, eh?'

'*Sir!*' Metzger bellowed. He raised his right hand to reveal that it was clad in a black glove.' The Ivans did for me, sir. The bone-menders said that I'd never be able to use it again.'

Von Dodenburg clicked his tongue sympathetically. 'Sorry about that, Metzger.'

1. General Kurt Student, chief of Germany's airborne troops.

'No matter, sir,' Metzger answered with false modesty. 'I'm one of the lucky ones. Just got to soldier on – that's all. Especially now when everybody's against us.'

Von Dodenburg nodded. 'Yes, you're right – we've all got to soldier on now. But do you think I could see the CO.'

'Of course, sir. But I'd better just check.'

Metzger turned and knocked very loudly on the inner door. He waited for what seemed a very long time, then stuck his head round the door carefully.

'Major von Dodenburg, sir,' he snapped.

'Let him come – in a moment, Metzger,' the Vulture's familiar voice rasped from within.

A moment later a small but beautiful young second-lieutenant in the Alpini came out of the inner office. In spite of the terrible heat, he had his greatcoat draped decoratively over his shoulders. He inclined his gleaming black head in von Dodenburg's direction.

'*Chiaou*', he muttered, flashing the German a tremendous white smile, and leaving behind him an overpowering odour of cologne.

'Who the hell is that?' von Dodenburg asked.

Metzger sniffed. 'That spaghetti-eater seems to have six more teeth than anybody else I know,' he grunted, but he did not enlighten von Dodenburg any further.

The Vulture rose immediately when von Dodenburg went in. His face seemed a little flushed and he was tugging at his jacket, as if something had just disarranged it.

'My dear von Dodenburg, how good to see you again – and congratulations on your promotion.'

'Thank you, sir.'

'And how's your head?'

'Getting better, the bone-menders say. But God knows how I got hit there. I was wearing my helmet after all.'

The Vulture offered him a seat. 'Good job, you did. Ap-

177

parently your tank bought it almost immediately, according to Schulze and the other chap who got you out. A minute later, my dear von Dodenburg, and you would not have got your promotion.'

'And Sergeant Schulze, what of him?'

'He seemed to have been badly wounded. He was bleeding severely at least when he brought you in. They bundled the lot of you in the ambulance and rushed you off to the rear.' He shrugged and fumbled with his flies which von Dodenburg noted were undone. 'He's probably in some damn base hospital, trying to get the bone-menders to release him. And just now, von Dodenburg, I can use every experienced NCO and officer I can lay my hands on, if I'm going to get this battle group on its feet before the Amis reach Rome.' He paused for a moment. 'Schwarz is back now by the way, though he has to report to Number Two Ospedale Militaire every day. They're fitting him up there with the arm. Luckily enough the Popovs shot off his left arm. Otherwise I wouldn't have been able to take him back.'

'Yes, lucky for him,' von Dodenburg said ironically.

'Schwarz'll be my adjutant. It'll be good to have him at my side because we're expanding very fast. As for you von Dodenburg, I'd like you to take over the Panzer Grenadier battalion in the Battle Group.'

'Thank you, sir. If we go on like this, we'll be a division before we know where we are,' von Dodenburg added with a laugh. But the Vulture did not return his laugh. He was deadly serious.

'That is exactly my plan, von Dodenburg. Now listen to what we're going to do . . .'

What followed was a race against time. The Allies landed at Salerno. Mussolini, the deposed Italian dictator, was found and rescued from his Italian captors by the paras and

178

an unknown SD man named Skorzeny. The Pact of Steel fell apart and in Rome the paras went into action against their one-time Allies. The Amis broke out of their Salerno bridgehead and drove for Naples. But otherwise events, as tremendous as they were, went unnoticed by the Vulture and his tiny staff.

One night the CO got the young captain commanding the paras guarding the HQ area drunk. The man had gained his jump wings back in 1941, but he still had to make his first combat jump. The Vulture worked on him all night. The next morning the disgruntled young para volunteered himself and his whole company for Battle Group Wotan.

With the aid of the beautiful young Lieutenant from the Alpini, the Vulture organised a squad to steal the demonstration company of Tigers which had been loaned to the Alpini at their training ground just outside Rome. Suddenly one morning, the men of Wotan woke up to find they were the possessors of ten brand-new Tigers, over which their officers sweated in the first rays of the sun to remove the Italian markings.

Schwarz was flown to the Wehrmacht's main military prison at Torgau and brought back with him half a company of 'volunteers' who preferred Wotan to the grim glasshouse and the possibility of a transfer to Penal Battalion 999. After the first deserter had been brought back and shot publicly by the Vulture himself, the 'Torgau Volunteers' settled down and attempted to soldier.

Von Dodenburg himself drove into the mountainous area around the northern city of Bolzano and brought back half a hundred big, rawboned Tyrolean farm boys who were officially Italian citizens, but who were as German as the Führer himself – although von Dodenburg could not understand a word they said when they spoke their own native dialect.

179

The new Battle Group took shape rapidly, though as Metzger was heard complaining more often than once, 'they're like the crappy Foreign Legion plus the crappy glasshouse cast-offs!' And indeed they were a very tough bunch, von Dodenburg thought as he watched them on the morning parades, very unlike the enthusiastic, idealistic young men who had flocked to the Wotan's standard in 1939. These men – paras, military criminals and veterans of the Citadel fiasco – had no illusions, no beliefs and no loyalty save to themselves and Battle Group Wotan.

'My dear von Dodenburg, 'the Vulture commented on one such morning as they marched off for training, 'to borrow a phrase from that Tommy general who helped our own Marshal Blucher to win the Battle of Waterloo, I don't know whether they'll frighten the enemy, but by God, they put the wind up me.'

Von Dodenburg had grinned. They 'put the wind up' him, too. But time was running out. All further recruiting stopped as did all training. The Battle Group went on Stage Two Alert. Hastily those of the new recruits who could drive or knew how to fire a cannon were placed in the Group's armoured component to fill the gaps in the Tiger crews; the rest were put into von Dodenburg's panzer grenadiers. As the Vulture remarked, tugging at the end of his great nose cynically:

'They'll train themselves after all. The ones who survive will be trained, and the ones who get their silly heads blown off will serve as an example to the others that it pays to learn one's job well in the SS.'

The younger officer was forced to agree: the situation in Southern Italy was far too serious to be worried about such trivia as training. The front could break down at any moment.

'Besides,' the Vulture added, 'everyone knows that the

Amis and the Tommies can't fight. Kill their officers and they run around in panic like chickens with their heads chopped off. After all it is common knowledge that the Anglo-Americans show very little initiative.'

But in spite of the weakness of the Battle Group's training, von Dodenburg worked flat out to ensure that his panzer grenadiers had the best possible equipment, returning to his billet at night blind with fatigue or when he couldn't sleep because of excessive fatigue, drinking himself into insensibility with one of the whores in the officers' brothel in the Mario di Fiori red light district.

On the day that the Tommy 8th Army joined up with the Amis east of Eboli and commenced the last phase of their attack on Naples, the Vulture assembled the Battle Group and told them they would be moving out to meet the enemy the following morning. Von Dodenburg flashed a look down the grey-clad ranks of his own panzer grenadiers. There seemed no reaction to the news. Most of the new recruits were still hungover from the night before's drinking bout and the clean-living farmboys from the Tyrol probably hadn't understood a word the Vulture had spoken in his clipped Prussian accent. Even if they had, he told himself with a faint grin, it would take another thirty minutes before the news penetrated their thick mountain brains.

The Vulture standing on an ammunition box in the centre of the ancient barracks square, surrounded by fine, florid Italian baroque buildings, squeezed in his monocle more firmly, and rasped:

'The morning will be devoted to packing the gear. The rest of the day is yours – and the night.' He smiled thinly, but there was no response from the Group.

Out of the corner of his eye, von Dodenburg caught a glimpse of bright canary yellow. The Alpini Lieutenant's

181

flashy Fiat sports car slid into the shade of the fine tall cypresses which bordered one side of the square. He waved lazily at the Vulture. The Vulture flushed lightly and went on faster:

'You may do as you wish. Two things, however – don't get the pox. I shall regard that as a court-martial offence and I don't need to tell you how self-inflicted wounds are punished in the present crisis. The other is – be back at zero six hundred hours, ready to march.' He grinned suddenly. 'Good hunting – and good shooting tonight. Dismiss!'

As Metzger supervised the march-off, von Dodenburg attempted to ask the Vulture for his orders for the day. But the CO had no time. His eyes were fixed strangely on the beautiful young officer waiting for him in the bright yellow car.

'Lothario is there,' he said thickly, 'and time is so short – so damnably short.' He strode off hurriedly, calling over his shoulder. 'If you have any questions, ask Schwarz!'

Thoughtfully von Dodenburg walked over to Schwarz. He looked at him significantly, but there was nothing but madness in his red eyes.

'Well, Schwarz,' he said. 'If the CO can do it, so can we. What about a drink and then the Mario di Fiori.'

'Anything you say, von Dodenburg.' He slapped his wooden hand against his pistol holster. 'As long as we are armed – one can't trust these Italians.'

Von Dodenburg laughed. 'I'm always armed, Schwarz when I go into the Mario di Fiori, but a little differently than you think.'

On the way to their quarters they met Metzger. He flung them a manificent salute, his right-hand jacket pocket bulging with worthless Lire notes for the girls in the red-light district:

'Permission to dismiss, sir?' he roared in his best sergeant-major fashion.

Von Dodenburg looked at him in mock severity. 'Dismiss, Sergeant Metzger! A good NCO is never off duty, especially in the Wotan. You can take over the Group office for the day. After all you'll be on a cushy number after today as a virtual non-combattant.' He indicated Metzger's gloved right hand. Metzger flushed, but said nothing. When they were safely out of earshot, however, he cursed thickly.

'Officers, I've shit em! A lot of pimps, poufs and pissing buck-passers; that's all the bastards are.' And with that he passed inside to give the duty clerks hell for the rest of that long September day.

The Mario di Fiori was doing booming business. Heavy-breasted, dark-eyed Italian whores with lazy hips and their skinny pimps in their uniform pin-striped suits were importuning the men in field-grey everywhere, as they wandered up and down the cobbled, grass-overgrown streets looking for adventure. Here and there there were long impatient queues of soldiers outside the official army brothels, which had been reserved for the Italian Army and which still charged the same low prices.

Just opposite there were equally long queues, supervised by hard-faced, suspicious-eyed 'chain dogs': men waiting to carry out the prescribed anti-VD treatment after having visited the whores, standing like so many animals at long zinc troughs to squirt wine-red potassium permanganate mixture into their penises to kill any possible infection.

The two SS officers swaggered through the waiting men, as if they were not there, and although the 'stubble-hoppers' grumbled they got out of the way swiftly enough.

'What I fancy,' von Dodenburg was just saying, 'is a nice little blonde – neat and trim and not too hefty like these

183

Italian women,' when they swung round the corner and bumped into the crowd of private soldiers, grouped round the women. Von Dodenburg broke off suddenly and gasped. He had rarely seen uglier women than the three who were the centre of the crowd. The first one was little more than a dwarf, her face as pale as death and her dark hair cropped, as if she had just escaped from a nunnery; the second was enormously fat and cross-eyed; whilst the third was a head taller than himself and had an enormous lump growing out of her right temple like a bullock's horn.

But it wasn't the three women who kept his attention; it was the voice of the man who was obviously their pimp. The man, dressed in rough civilian clothes, had his back to them as he praised the sexual talents of his three 'mares', as he kept calling them to the laughing soldiers. But there was no mistaking that cheeky waterfront voice.

'I calls them Faith, Hope and Charity,' he was saying. 'The little short-arsed one here, she's Faith because she doesn't spread them for money. No, not at all! She's more a – you might say – charitable institution – she wants your green leaves [1] so that you won't spend it on the demon drink. She gives it to the Pope – personally! As for Hope here, the one with the four-eyes – you know you could put yer head between them knockers on her and think you was deaf – she's hoping that a real man will come along one of these days who's got a whanger big enough to get close to her and give her a real thrill.' He lowered his voice confidentially. 'You wouldn't believe it, but it's true – she's still a virgin!'

'*Schulze!*' von Dodenburg bellowed, finding his voice at last.

The pimp swung round as if he had been shot, his forefinger still raised in praise of his 'mares'. The ruddiness had gone from his face and he had a fresh, livid scar over his

1. Army slang for money (transl.)

right eye, but there was no mistaking him. It was Schulze all right.

His mouth dropped open as he muttered, 'Great crap on the Christmas Tree, it's Captain von Dodenburg...'

Schwarz had departed upstairs with Faith. Schulze took a deep swig at his red wine and then licking his suddenly dry lips launched into his story.

'You see it was like this, sir. By the way congratulations on your promotion—'

'Get on with it, Schulze,' von Dodenburg interrupted threateningly. 'None of your soft soap.'

'Well, we'd rescued you from the Tiger, with that nasty bang on the head you got. As soon as we managed to get you to a dressing station, they decided to keep us too. We were both hit, me and Hartmann. And a couple of twenty rouble pieces didn't hurt either. So all three of us was whipped on the Red Cross train to Lvov General Hospital.'

'That's where I woke up,' Von Dodenburg said. Above his head the springs of Faith's bed were creaking mightily. 'But you weren't there. Nor Hartmann.'

'No, sir, well you see we decided that we might get cured quicker and return sooner to the Battalion if we received treatment in the Reich. You know how it is? Anyway we got to Munich and we sort of decided there that we should go south. A doctor we got to know at the military hospital in Schwabing said the air would heal our wounds sooner in Austria and we did want to get back to the Battalion. He signed the paper assigning us to the hospital at Bad Ischl. And then we was out for a walk one day, we must have missed our way and there we were in spaghetti-land. Of course, we wanted to come straight back. But we thought one day more or less wouldn't do any harm. I always heard that Italy's a great place for culture. Didn't Schiller come down here or something?' He looked at von Dodenburg inquiringly.

'Goethe,' the officer corrected.

'Well, I knew it was one of them singers a long time back. So we thought what was good enough for them was good enough for us.' Above them the squeaking of the rusty bedsprings had stopped, but little bits of plaster were still drifting down on their heads.

'Well, go on,' von Dodenburg prompted. 'How did your excursion into culture land you in your present – er – business?' He pointed a finger upwards.

'It was Hartmann, sir. The bastard, if you'll forgive the expression? He wanted to look at the boats at Genoa.'

'You mean you two rogues wanted to desert!'

'I wouldn't put it as drastic as that, sir. It was just that we thought a trip to Spain or somewhere like that would speed up our recovery. All we had in mind was getting back to the mob as soon as possible. Well, at least that's what *I* had in mind. It was different with Hartmann.'

'How?'

Schulze touched the new scar on his forehead. 'The same night that we made contact with a Spanish skipper, the bastard whopped me on the head. I was unconscious for twelve hours. When I woke up, he was gone and the roubles too.'

'Well, why didn't you report to the nearest military police post?' von Dodenburg asked sharply.

'I was ashamed, sir,' Schulze said and hung his head. 'After all, I'd been trying all along to get cured so that I could get back to my unit and now here I was with my head bashed in again, no use to anybody again.'

Von Dodenburg could hear Schwarz's heavy boots coming down the rickety stairs; he had to make a decision fast. 'All right, Schulze, *SS Man* Schulze, I'll say no more about

186

your desertion. You'll lose your rank and return as a common soldier. Wotan is full of rogues now, one more won't make any difference, I suppose.'

Schulze raised his head. His light blue eyes were sparkling, as of old.

'You won't regret it, sir,' he said enthusiastically.

'I know, I won't, Schulze. The next time it'll be the firing squad. Now get rid of those mares of yours and report back to the Battalion at once. I'm sure Sergeant Metzger will be pleased to see you again.'

'Just one request, sir, before I go.'

'What?' von Dodenburg asked impatiently.

'Well, sir.' Schulze was suddenly hesitant. 'The girls have done well by me this last month. I don't think it would be right just to leave them like that. I mean it wouldn't, would it?'

'Get on with it, man!'

'Well, I think I ought to slip them a last link. Not Faith because she'll still have wet decks from Captain Schwarz. But the other two – Hope and Charity. I mean, sir, they love me.'

Major von Dodenburg exploded. 'Schulze, you're an impossible rogue. Get back to those bloody barracks before I change my mind and have you shot here and now!'

Naples was burning. Somewhere miles out to sea the great enemy battleships pounded the Italian port with their massive sixteen inch guns. They couldn't see them, but every time the Amis fired, the horizon erupted in a series of volcanoes. They were supported by flight after flight of twin-engined Mitchells which dropped tons of bombs on even the smallest hamlet bordering Highway Six, the vital road leading north to Cassino and from thence to Rome.

But Battle Group Wotan was well dug in. Von Dodenburg's panzer grenadiers were scattered on both sides of the highway as it straightened and began to run towards the bridge across the River Volturno, while the Vulture's Tigers were carefully concealed, hull down, on the right bank of the river itself. When the Amis finally took the crossroads up ahead and began to roll north again, they would be in for a great surprise.

The first stubble-hopper from one of the scratch infantry battalions defending the highway came tearing up, his eyes wide, staring and crazed with fear. He burst through their foxholes, crying:

'They're coming . . . they're coming, thousands of them!'

They didn't attempt to stop him. He was a broken man, no use to them. Besides the chain dogs had thrown a barricade across the road beyond the bridge to stop people like the panic-stricken stubble-hopper. They would shoot him without trial as an example to those who would undoubtedly follow. And they did. A good half hundred of them, their arms flailing wildly as they fought to make their escape, throwing away their weapons in their blind panic. Again the panzer grenadiers, crouched pale-faced and tense in their coffinlike holes, let them run by without hindrance. One of the ex-paras spat drily and remarked contemptuously:

'Typical Greater German infantry – the first enemy shell and they wet their field-grey knickers.'

Five minutes later the Ami artillery bombardment swamped them. It seemed the Amis had an inexhaustible supply of shells. They worked over the whole area beyond the cross-roads, switching their fire back and forth suddenly, as if the fire-control officers were hoping to catch the enemy in the opening. But they didn't. Von Dodenburg's panzer grenadiers were cowering deep inside their narrow pits, tense bodies pulled into the foetal position, as the red-hot shrapnel hissed harmlessly over them.

At last it stopped. Cautiously they peered over the edges of their pits. The landscape in front of them had been transformed, as if a hundred gigantic moles had been at work in a sudden frenzy of digging. Anxiously von Dodenburg asked for casualties. With relief he heard that they only amounted to six and ten wounded.

'Put the dead in one of the shell holes and send the walking wounded back to Group HQ,' he ordered and settled down to wait again at Schulze's side, as he crouched there over his spandau.

Time passed leadenly. To their front all was silent. Nothing moved save for the smoke streaming straight upwards into the blue Italian sky from the burning crossroads.

'Think the Amis must have gone back home for a bit to eat and one of them milk shakes they were always drinking in the pictures before the war,' Schulze said and wiped the sweat off his face.

'It's a nice thought, Schulze, but somehow I think the gentlemen from America will be paying us a visit before this day is much older.'

'Could be,' Schulze said morosely. 'Could be.' Then his big face brightened. 'Did I ever tell you the joke about the bras they issue to the 'field mattresses', sir?'

'No,' von Dodenburg said, not taking his eyes off the wide valley of the Volturno in front of him. 'No, I don't believe you ever did, Schulze.'

'Well, sir. There are five sizes – small, medium, large. Then there's – wow, holy God!' He paused dramatically for the punch line. 'And then, there's – my aching back—'

'Shut up!' von Dodenburg snapped. 'Here they come!' He raised his voice. 'Pass the word – stand to your weapons everybody! The gentlemen from America are here.'

As his panzer grenadiers fumbled with their weapons and took aim, von Dodenburg watched the first khaki-clad figures emerge cautiously from the burning crossroads, their rifles held defensively across their chests, walking on the balls of their feet fearfully, as if they expected a slug to whack into their soft flesh at any moment. They would be the scouts, he decided. The handful clambered up the embankment onto the white, pitted road and began to advance up it warily. Now more and more Amis came into view behind them. Suddenly the fields and olive groves on both sides filled with plodding cautious khaki figures. Even more of them. Scores, hundreds, thousands. They were so thick on the shattered ground that they formed almost solid lines.

'Holy shit!' Schulze breathed at his side, as he lifted his spandau, adjusted the long belt of ammunition and then tucked the wooden butt firmly into his shoulder. 'There must be thousands of the bastards! Amis everywhere. They must breed like shitting rabbits in the United States of shitting America!'

Von Dodenburg did not comment. All of a sudden he felt old. There had been many other moments just like this in the past four years: first the Belgies, then the Frogs. After them the Tommies and the Popovs. Now the new boys – the Amis.

'Breed like shitting rabbits,' Schulze had said. It seemed like that. As if all over the world, hatred and envy of Germany spawned new enemies. Kill them as they might, there were always fresh enemies to take the place of the dead ones. He was seized by an irrespressible desire to see the faces of these new enemies, who had come nearly five thousand kilometres to be slaughtered on this hot Italian plain. He lifted his binoculars and focused them on the first line of American infantry, sweeping the glass along their faces.

They were fresh, well-fed and unlined. Most of them were young, and one or two of them appeared to be laughing or joking, as if the advance were a walk-over, a simple stroll under the bright Italian sun; as if their real war would be fought by machines and not human beings. He stared transfixed at them. They were the faces of innocence, still untouched by the compromise, the brutalities, the horrors of total war. They made him feel very old – and very angry.

He dropped his binoculars. With a bound he sprang onto the top of the foxhole so that his men could see him clearly. He raised his hand in signal. The panzer grenadiers - criminals, paras, mountain boys and veterans – squinted through their sights at the carelessly advancing Amis.

'Welcome to Europe – Americans!' von Dodenburg screamed with rage. He brought his hand down sharply.

Schulze squeezed the trigger of his spandau. With a jolting high-pitched scream it burst into deadly life. White-and-red tracer zipped across the valley. The next instant the rest of the panzer grenadier line erupted. Lead cut the air. Amis began dropping, faces contorted with horror, pain and surprise. Wotan's new battle with a new enemy had commenced.